Goddess Girls

MEDUSA
THE MEAN

Goddess Girls

MEDUSA
THE MEAN

JOAN HOLUB & SUZANNE WILLIAMS

Aladdin

NEW YORK   LONDON   TORONTO   SYDNEY   NEW DELHI

ALADDIN

An imprint of Simon & Schuster Children's Publishing Division
1230 Avenue of the Americas, New York, NY 10020
First Aladdin hardcover edition December 2013
Cover illustration copyright © 2012 by Glen Hanson
Text copyright © 2012 by Joan Holub and Suzanne Williams
Also available in an Aladdin paperback edition.
For information about special discounts for bulk purchases,
please contact Simon & Schuster Special Sales at 1-866-506-1949
or business@simonandschuster.com.
The Simon & Schuster Speakers Bureau can bring authors to your live event.
For more information or to book an event contact the Simon & Schuster Speakers
Bureau at 1-866-248-3049 or visit our website at www.simonspeakers.com.
Designed by Karin Paprocki
The text of this book was set in Baskerville Handcut Regular.
Manufactured in the United States of America 1113 FFG
2 4 6 8 10 9 7 5 3 1
Library of Congress Control Number 2012930494
ISBN 978-1-4424-8595-2 (hc)
ISBN 978-1-4424-3379-2 (pbk)
ISBN 978-1-4424-3380-9 (eBook)

CONTENTS

Prologue

THE KIDS IN SIX-YEAR-OLD MEDUSA GORGON'S first grade class at Aegean Elementary School in Greece had made fun of her again today. They'd called her Gorgonzola Head. They'd pinched their noses and said she smelled like stinky cheese. But now that school was over and Medusa was home in her bedroom, she pulled out her favorite green crayon and a sheet of papyrus to draw on. At the top, she wrote:

The Queen of Mean:

A hilarious and very exactly true

comic strip about me, Medusa!

"In today's episode," little Medusa began as she started drawing stick figures with big round heads, "those doo-doo-nose kids who teased me at school get clobbered by me and my magic—for I am the Queen of Mean! Yayyyy! And *nobody* messes with me and gets away with it."

Tucking her tongue to one side of her mouth, Medusa concentrated on drawing herself yelling at the other kids. "It's payback time, losers! Because you teased me, now I'm going to bonk you all on the head."

Then she drew herself bonking them with her secret weapon, a big yellow magic cheese. In a speech bubble by her mouth, she wrote her magic word: *Gorgonzola!* In the next frame, all the kids who'd made fun of

her had been turned into cheese. Ha-ha-ha!

"Next, I—the Queen of Mean—run home to my mom and dad," Medusa said under her breath. "And guess what. They have been magically turned into smiley parents who hug me."

Medusa drew the scene with quick strokes of her crayon. There was her mom and now her dad, looking at her with big, happy grins. Beside them she drew two girls who looked just like her, because they were triplets.

"And then the Queen's sisters, who didn't help when these kids made fun of her, find out they've got cooties," she continued. "So now they are banished to the doghouse forever, and the Queen gets to have their big, beautiful room all to herself. Awesome!"

Then she wrote: *The end.*

Medusa gazed happily at her finished comic strip. If only things in her real life could turn out so perfectly!

3

1

Seven Years Later

FROM HER SEAT HIGH AT THE BACK OF THE stone bleachers in the outdoor amphitheater at Mount Olympus Academy, thirteen-year-old Medusa stared in fascination at a full-page ad in her new *Teen Scrollazine*. It showed a picture of a sparkly necklace with a golden-winged white horse charm dangling from its chain. Her pale green eyes eagerly devoured the sales pitch:

At the bottom of the page was an order form.

Becoming immortal had been Medusa's dearest wish since—well, since forever. It wasn't fair that her two sisters were immortal while *she'd* been born a mere mortal.

She studied the ad again. She wanted to believe it, but did she dare trust its claims? What if it was a trick? Could a flying-horse necklace really be the key to immortality? "Doubt it!" she muttered aloud.

6

A godboy sitting nearby overheard and gave her a sideways glance. She shot him a quick glare that widened his eyes and made him nervously look away.

It was Friday, last period, and the amphitheater was filled with immortal students—all of them beautiful, powerful, and awesome, with softly glittering skin. How she longed to be like them!

Sure, she went to MOA too. She was one of the few lucky mortals allowed to attend the Academy. Yet she had no true magical powers, like those of a goddess. Still, with a glance she *could* turn a mortal to stone. That was something, at least. And she was the only student with snakes instead of hair growing from the top of her head! Glancing around, she idly reached up and twirled one of the snakes around her finger.

Usually school dramas were performed in the amphitheater, but today the entire student body had gathered here because of Career-ology Week. (Or *Job-ology* Week, as the students called it.) All week long various speakers had come to MOA to talk about their jobs. Yesterday the god Hermes had told them all about his chariot delivery service.

Today the goddess Hera was here speaking about her wedding shop in the Immortal Marketplace. The regal-looking goddess had thick blond hair styled high upon her head and a no-nonsense look in her eye. Although she wasn't unusually tall, something about her made her seem statuesque. Probably her confidence.

As Hera explained how she went about planning a wedding at Hera's Happy Endings, Medusa only half-listened. She shifted behind some other MOA students sitting in front of her, so she was better hidden from Hera's view.

Sneakily she re-read the ad. It was maddeningly short

on details about how the Immortalizer worked—if it worked at all. She'd almost be willing to risk disappointment if only it didn't cost so much. Thirty drachmas was a lot of money! Her weekly allowance was just three obeloi, which was half a drachma. At the moment she only had eight drachmas saved up.

"Any questions?" Hera asked the crowd.

Medusa jolted to attention and peered around the godboy in front of her. Seeing that the talk was nearly over, she set her scrollazine on the bench. Although the bleachers were packed with students, there was an empty space on either side of her. No one ever got too close to a girl with snake hair.

Since class participation counted for a third of her Job-ology grade, she quickly tried to think up a question. But how could she when she hadn't heard a word Hera had said!

Medusa rolled her eyes when Athena raised her hand. What a Goody Two-sandals! She was always the first to ask questions in class. Athena was not only the brainiest girl at MOA, she was also Principal Zeus's daughter. And soon she'd be Hera's stepdaughter too, because Zeus and Hera were getting married in nine days—just a week from Sunday.

Medusa craned her neck to look at Zeus. He was in the audience, sitting front row center, gazing adoringly at Hera. They'd announced their engagement not long ago during the boys' Olympic Games. Now the whole school was abuzz with the news of their upcoming marriage.

"Who will your bridesmaids be?" Athena asked when she was called on.

"I'm not sure yet," Hera replied. "Since we've decided to follow tradition, Zeus will be choosing seven boys as groomsmen, and they will in turn choose seven brides-maids. Any other questions?"

Athena's shoulders drooped, and her long brown hair swayed in an annoyingly cute, curly way as she slowly shook her head. She had to be less than thrilled with this answer. She'd probably thought she had a clear shot at becoming a bridesmaid.

Another goddessgirl asked a question. Then pale, mysterious Persephone asked about the flowers for the wedding. Apparently her mom's flower shop would be providing them.

Next Aphrodite—the most beautiful goddessgirl at MOA—waved her hand in the air. Even from high up in the bleachers, Medusa could see that Aphrodite's per-fectly manicured fingernails were polished a sparkly robin's-egg-blue that matched the chiton she wore. As Medusa squinted at the goddessgirl's fingernails, the color of the polish changed, first to turquoise, then pink, then back to blue. *Must be nice to possess magic that makes your nail polish change colors,* she thought sourly. Goddessgirls took that kind of thing for granted.

"What will your gown look like?" Aphrodite asked when called on.

Ye gods, thought Medusa. Not that she cared, but what did these questions have to do with Job-ology, anyway? They were all *personal* questions! Tuning out Hera's answer, she realized that almost all the girls seemed mesmerized by this froufrou marriage stuff. It made sense for Aphrodite, since she was the goddessgirl of love. But why were the others so interested? She didn't get it.

She watched the sun catch in Aphrodite's long golden hair as the goddessgirl tucked a curl behind one ear. It was a trademark Aphrodite move that drew boys' eyes like a magnet. Although Medusa had tried to do it with her snake hair once, it just didn't have the same effect.

At least dark-haired Artemis, who sat one row below Medusa, seemed a little bored. She had dumped some arrows out of her quiver and was checking their tips for wear. Medusa could relate. This whole marriage thing was a big yawn. She'd be glad when it was over.

Medusa had carefully chosen her spot on the bleachers today. Studying Athena, Persephone, Aphrodite, and Artemis—the most popular goddessgirls in school— was practically her full-time job, though she made sure no one ever noticed. And although she'd never admit it, she was green with envy when it came to those four. Literally. Her skin, eyes, and hair were *all* green.

Besides immortality, there were just two other things she wanted in life: to be as effortlessly popular as the four goddessgirls and to have her supercrush suddenly decide he liked her. Unfortunately, both seemed way out of reach. She didn't trust anyone enough to let down her guard with them and become friends. And how can you be popular without friends? As far as her crush went, well . . .

"My turn!" a nearby godboy said to his friends in an excited but muted tone. She'd know that voice anywhere. *Poseidon.* Oh-so-casually she looked his way. He was sitting three rows down from her with two other godboys— Dionysus and Ares. Weddings obviously didn't interest them either, since they were secretly playing a game of Javelin Thump.

Poseidon was carefully aiming a piece of papyrus that had been folded into a fat triangle about two inches on its long side. As she watched, he flicked it across the seat with his middle finger. "Score!" he exclaimed in a whisper as the triangle slid between Dionysus's two fingers, which marked the goalposts. His flick had been so strong, however, that the little triangle javelin kept on going. There was a mad scramble to grab it before it slid off the edge of the boys' bench, but they weren't fast enough. It dropped onto the ground by their feet.

Before the boys could catch her watching them, Medusa made herself look away. Still, if she could've gotten away with it, she would've stared at blond, turquoise-eyed Poseidon all day long. Feeling someone's gaze, she glanced up into a pair of violet eyes. For some reason, Dionysus was looking at her now. Assuming the worst, she peeked down, checking to be sure her underwear wasn't showing.

"If there are no further questions . . ." said Hera, snagging Medusa's attention once more.

Uh-oh! She still hadn't spoken up. Quickly she raised her hand.

"Yes?" Hera had to crane her neck to look up at her.

"Why do goddesses need jobs?" Medusa asked. "They're goddesses, after all. They don't *need* to work; they can do whatever they want!"

Hera smiled, her blond hair gleaming in the afternoon sun. "Whether you're a goddess or a shopkeeper, being happy is all about finding your personal strengths and using them to do what you enjoy—be it work or not."

Without waiting to be called on again, Medusa blurted, "But what happens when a goddess weds? Surely Principal Zeus won't want you to continue to run Hera's Happy Endings once you're married. How would you have time?"

Students nearby gasped at her bluntness. She felt Athena glare at her. But she was used to being on the receiving end of glares. She'd never been exactly popular. Far from it, in fact. Stirring up trouble and making others uncomfortable were abilities that came naturally to her. They were her *strengths*. She wondered what kind of job Hera would suggest she use that talent for!

Seeming unfazed, Hera answered her, polite as always. "That's a goddess's choice, but I do plan to continue working in my shop."

At her reply Zeus frowned darkly and crossed his arms. Wide gold bands flashed at his wrists. After taking a few more questions, Hera left the stage. Zeus joined her, gesturing like he was trying to convince her of something as they headed off. At seven feet tall with bulging muscles, wild red hair, piercing blue eyes, and a fearsome temper, he usually got his way in any argument. Medusa wondered if he would succeed this time.

Now that the lecture was over, students began to exit the bleachers. Medusa dawdled, waiting for the others below her to leave before she stood. Stepping down two rows of seats, she pretended to accidentally drop her

Teen Scrollazine under the bench where Poseidon had sat. She stooped and reached for the papyrus javelin that he and his friends had left behind. Tucking it in the pocket of her chiton, she then picked up her scrollazine and straightened—only to find Aphrodite standing in front of her.

Startled, Medusa jumped. All twelve of her snakes hissed in surprise. "Give me a heart attack, why don't you?" she said in annoyance.

Stepping back, Aphrodite eyed the snakes warily, but then her face took on a determined look. "We're going out for ambrosia shakes and snacks at the Supernatural Market later. Everyone's talking about wedding gift ideas for Hera and Zeus. Want to come with us?"

Godness! She never should have told the truth a few weeks ago when Aphrodite had asked why she didn't like her. What Medusa had replied was something like,

"Everything's so easy for you just because you're pretty. You don't even have to try, and boys adore you. It's not fair." She hoped Aphrodite didn't feel sorry for her because of that, but she had a feeling she did. Because now Aphrodite was always trying to be fake-friendly and include her in things. Medusa was sure she and the other goddessgirls didn't really want her butting in.

"Sorry. I'm busy," Medusa replied tartly, even though she did kind of want to hang out with them.

Aphrodite put a hand on one hip, like she didn't believe her. "Doing what?"

"Stuff." Medusa's fingers toyed with the papyrus javelin in her pocket. She really did have something to do, but she wasn't about to tell Aphrodite what it was. Because it was a big secret!

2
Medusa's Big Secret

As MEDUSA STARTED EDGING OUT OF THE
row of bleachers, Aphrodite stayed put. "Come by later
if you change your m—," she called out.

"Yeah, okay," Medusa interrupted, not waiting for
her to finish. After zipping down the stone steps, she
dashed off toward the dorms. She didn't trust Aphrodite's sudden offer of friendship. And she didn't

need anyone to befriend her out of pity!

When she got to her room on the fourth floor of the Academy, she unlocked it, rushed inside, and then closed the door. *Click!* She locked it behind her. As far as she knew, she was the only girl in the dorms who'd put a lock on her door. But she wasn't about to trust her privacy to the honor system like everyone else. No one but she had been inside this room since third grade. Not even her two sisters, Stheno and Euryale. And she planned to keep it that way.

Tossing the *Teen Scrollazine* onto her desk beside a stack of textscrolls from her classes, Medusa then went to kneel on her spare bed. Like all the other dorm rooms, hers had two twin beds on opposite sides of the room, and two desks, but only one of each was used. Oh, she'd had roommates in the past. But she'd driven them off, one by one.

In third grade she'd been paired with a mortal named Pandora. That girl had been nothing but constant questions. Medusa had quickly figured out how to drive her away, though. She'd just answered her questions with more questions. Like if Pandora said, "Have you done your homework?" Medusa would answer, "Why do you ask?" If Pandora said, "Do you think Poseidon is cute?" Medusa would reply, "Do *you* think he's cute?" Finally the curious girl couldn't take it anymore and requested a room reassignment. She was Athena's problem now.

Her next roommate had been Pheme, the goddess-girl of gossip. She had a weird habit of puffing her words into the air in little clouds, so you could read them. She couldn't help it, but Medusa had coughed and complained, finally declaring the room a no-smoking zone and refusing to let Pheme speak. Since the girl lived to gossip, it had practically killed her to stay quiet. Finally she'd moved out too. Nowadays Medusa had the whole room all to herself. Just the way she liked it.

She reached into her pocket and pulled out the little triangular javelin she'd picked up in the bleachers. Staring at the giant bulletin board on her wall next to the bed, she searched for a place to pin it. Eventually she fastened it between the pine-gum wrapper Poseidon had dropped on the playground in third grade and the comic he'd drawn of Mr. Cyclops back in fourth-grade Hero-ology class. *There!*

She stood back and gazed at the tribute to her super-crush that she'd created. This was her big secret!

Her bulletin board held every single thing Poseidon had ever touched and left behind in her presence. There were Oracle-O cookie fortunes that she'd sneaked from his lunch trays after he'd set them in the cafeteria tray return. There was a napkin he had dropped at the Hero

Week dance. On it he'd scribbled a few lines of a song he was writing for Heavens Above, the band he was in with some other godboys. And around the edges of the board, she'd arranged pictures of him she'd cut out of *Teen Scrollazine* over the years. He'd been the first boy to say hi to her on her first day at MOA, and she'd liked him ever since.

In fact, he was in her head so much that she could almost hear his voice now. Wait a sec. That *was* his voice!

She hurried over to her window and peered down into the courtyard. There he was, walking toward the sports fields along with Apollo, Ares, and a few girls, including Pandora! Everyone knew she was crushing on Poseidon too.

Pandora said something, and Poseidon laughed. But then another girl spoke, and he turned his attention to her. From the way he acted, Medusa could never tell if he liked Pandora or not. He had danced with her a lot at the last school dance. But then, he flirted with just about every girl in sight. And he always got away with it because he was so cute and fascinating. Even Athena had seemed interested in him when she'd first enrolled at MOA earlier in the year. Fortunately, if she had liked him then, the feeling appeared to have blown over.

Medusa cringed as Poseidon laughed at something Pandora said yet again. This was all Aphrodite's fault. Medusa had hinted like crazy that she wanted to be fixed up with Poseidon at the Hero Week dance. But instead, clueless Aphrodite had paired her with Dionysus. *Humph!* Some goddess of love she was!

Medusa had gone along with it, just to see what would happen. But although Dionysus was cute and all, he wasn't serious about anything. And that made him practically the opposite of her. Besides, he'd worn a stupid blindfold the whole time they'd danced. She was pretty sure he hadn't guessed she was his partner.

Still, she'd heard the snarky whispers around her even though she'd pretended not to. "He put on a blindfold so he wouldn't have to look at her." A tiny spear of hurt pierced her at the memory, but she pushed it away. Who cared what they thought?

One of her snakes gently head-bumped her cheek as if to offer comfort. "Hungry, guys?" she asked. "Who wants snake snacks?" Grabbing the extra ambrosia burger she'd stuffed into her bag at lunch and the snake snack sack from her closet, she went to sit at her desk.

With a sigh she opened her textscroll for Beauty-ology class, her worst subject. "Time to hit the scrolls," she murmured to herself. As she eased into study mode, she alternated taking a bite of her burger with tossing a bunch of dried peas and carrots high overhead. Her snakes quickly snapped these up before they could drop to the ground. Unlike most snakes, hers were vegetarians.

A while later she heard the voices of Athena, Aphrodite, Persephone, and Artemis in the hallway. Heading out for the Supernatural Market, probably. She sighed again, feeling a little sorry for herself. She was likely the only student at MOA who was studying tonight. Everyone else was out having fun. You'd think she'd be used to it by now, though.

She'd had to work extra hard to keep up with the immortals ever since coming to MOA in third grade. This was her second biggest secret. Only she knew how many hours she had to study—in private—to keep her grades up. It was the real reason she had turned down Aphrodite's offer to hang out tonight.

Truth was, she struggled with her studies. She'd die if anyone ever found that out. In fact, sometimes—like today—she purposely goofed off in class, doing stuff like reading a scrollazine just to make everyone think her good grades were effortless.

The few other mortals at MOA, such as Pandora and Heracles, didn't seem to have much problem keeping up. But maybe they weren't cursed with dim-witted blockheads for parents like she was. Although Medusa's mom and dad had gotten tutors for her immortal sisters, they'd actively discouraged *her* from bothering with an education.

"Why don't you quit school and get a job carrying water to and from the community well like your friends here on Earth," they'd said. But Medusa hadn't listened. No, instead she had followed her sisters to MOA, determined to get an education. She had aspirations for herself. Nobody was going to keep her down!

Still, minutes later, when she heard the four goddess-girls chatting below in the courtyard, she went to the window to wistfully watch them slip on their magic sandals and skim out of sight. On their way to have tons of fun, no doubt.

Just imagine if she were a goddess too, she thought. Life would be easy-peasy. She'd have magical powers and could boss mortals around, and they would have to worship her! And if she were immortal, she'd have a better chance at getting the two things she wanted most. Her supercrush and popularity!

How perfect would that be? Very.

Going back to her desk, she picked up the *Teen Scrollazine* and stared at the ad for the Immortalizer again. At the very bottom of the page were testimonials from satisfied customers who'd supposedly tried it.

"TRUST ME. THIS THING WORKS!" *–PEITHO*

"IT'S AMAZING. NO LIE!" *–APATE*

Sure, it seemed too good to be true, but what if the necklace really did work? What if she *could* become immortal?

The golden wings on the horse charm in the picture sparkled, as if beckoning her to buy. She knew it was probably dumb to think she might get immortality via mail order, but she felt desperate. Her chances with Poseidon seemed to be slipping away, and after years at MOA she was nowhere close to becoming popular.

Determination filled her. She tore out the order form for the Immortalizer, grabbed a feather pen, and began to fill it out. She was going to make her dreams come true—one way or another!

There was just one big problem. She didn't have enough money to buy the necklace. But she knew who probably did.

3
Mail-Order Immortality

I NEED A LOAN," MEDUSA ANNOUNCED AS SHE took the empty seat across from her two sisters at their cafeteria table the next morning. After getting dressed and feeding her snakes, she'd knocked at their dorm room door, found them gone, and then tracked them here.

"What kind? A sense of humor loan?" asked Stheno. Although the three of them were triplets—all with green skin—only her sisters' skin shimmered. Being immortal, they were goddessgirls, of course. A fact they liked to remind her of often.

Euryale grinned. "Or maybe a brain loan?"

"Ha-ha," said Medusa, pouring honey milk on a bowl of Ambrosia Flakes. Just because they were immortal and older than her by a few measly minutes, they liked to act as if they were way superior. "But really—I need money. Twenty-two drachmas, to be exact."

"Huh? What for?" asked Euryale.

Medusa studied her cereal before taking a spoonful. Although she ate the same stuff that godboys and god-dessgirls did, it didn't make her skin sparkle and didn't give her any special powers. Unfortunately.

Maybe she should just tell her sisters the truth, she mused, staring at the floating flakes. You never knew. When she least expected it, they'd act all nice and help her out. After all, she wouldn't have even gotten into MOA in the first place if they hadn't sneaked her in that first day of school.

The front office clerk, Ms. Hydra, had been confused when they'd shown up at the Academy—three identical girls barely eight years old. She'd checked her admissions scroll, saying, "I only have two Gorgon sisters on my list. Principal Zeus's invitation was for twins, not triplets."

"Must be a mistake," Medusa had piped up. "I'm their sister—a goddessgirl, just like them. See?" Pointing a finger, she'd magically lifted a textscroll from the counter and twirled it around to convince the clerk she was telling the truth. Of course, her sisters had been the ones who'd actually secretly performed the magic.

But by the time the girls' trick had been discovered weeks later, Medusa was already attending classes at MOA and making good grades. Fortunately, Zeus appreciated a good trick (he was famed for them on Earth), so he'd allowed Medusa to stay.

"Earth to snakehead," said Stheno, snapping her fingers to get Medusa's attention.

Medusa batted her hand away and then took a bite of cereal. Everyone at school probably thought she and her sisters were best buds. But Stheno and Euryale were much closer to each other than to her. They liked being more powerful than she was, so she seriously doubted they'd help her become a goddessgirl too. And that's why she couldn't tell them the real reason she needed a loan.

Racking her brain, she tried to think of some other explanation that would convince her moneybags sisters to fork over some cash. Suddenly two of her snakes swooped down in front of her face. They tied themselves into a bow as if wrapped around a present.

What do presents have to do with anything? Medusa

34

wondered. Then one of her snakes formed itself into a zigzag shape, so it looked like one of Zeus's thunderbolts. And lightning fast, an idea hit her.

Thanks, guys, she mouthed silently. She glanced at her sisters. "I need the money to buy a wedding present for Hera and Zeus," she fibbed.

"Use your allowance," said Euryale.

Medusa sat back in her chair, folding her arms. "You get three times more allowance than I do." It was true. Their mom and dad liked her sisters more. "And since worshipful mortals are always giving stuff to goddesses, you hardly ever have to buy anything yourselves. You must have a ton of money saved by now. C'mon."

"No can do," said Stheno, smirking.

"Pretty please with nectar on top? I'll pay you back." She wasn't beyond begging when she had to.

"Nuh-uh," said Euryale, shaking her head. "Sorry."

Medusa straightened and jabbed her spoon into her bowl in annoyance. It was hard always having to be dependent on her sisters' goodwill. They usually only helped her when it somehow benefited them.

Hey! That was it! She needed to make it seem that giving her money would be in their best interest.

Thinking quickly, she said, "Okay, but you know it'll make you look bad if your little sister doesn't have a gift for the wedding, right? I'll think of something, though. Maybe I'll just knit some socks for Zeus and Hera, or make them a jar of pomegranate jam." She sighed, rubbing it in. "Of course that'll look pretty pathetic compared to a gift like the magical golden apples a godboy like Hephaestus can make."

Stheno and Euryale exchanged glances. Ha! She had them worried now. Victory was near, Medusa thought, innocently munching her cereal.

Euryale leaned forward with her elbows on the table. "Okay, *little sister,* tell you what we'll do. If you promise to clean our room, we'll take you to the Immortal Marketplace today to shop for a decent gift."

"And the loan?" Medusa asked hopefully.

"Don't push your luck," said Stheno. "We'll think about it."

"Okay, deal," Medusa agreed.

Euryale cackled with laughter. "Ha-ha-ha! We were going there anyway!"

Medusa shrugged. She'd already guessed as much. But if they all hung out together, she'd have more time to try to squeeze some money out of them.

Minutes later the three sisters finished breakfast, stowed their trays in the return, and then headed out of the cafeteria. On their way out they passed some godboys at a nearby table laughing like crazy.

"Can you believe this?" asked Ares, nudging Apollo and handing him an open *Teen Scrollazine*. Apollo skimmed it, then laughed too. "Godsamighty! Mortals will try anything to become like us," he said.

From a distance Medusa couldn't read the page, but she could see it had a sparkly winged horse on it. Obviously they were making fun of the Immortalizer ad. Their reaction didn't change her mind one bit about buying the gadget, though. Immortals were always poking fun at mortals for wanting to be like them. They just didn't know how lucky they were!

Aphrodite and Athena walked into the cafeteria just as Medusa and her sisters were going out. When both of them smiled at Medusa and seemed about to speak, she pretended not to see them and sped up to get away. *What is up with those goddessgirls lately?* she wondered. Their niceness was weirding her out.

Still, a tiny part of her wondered what might have happened if she'd said hi back? Oh, well. Too late now. Besides, what if they'd only looked surprised and replied, *We weren't talking to* you. How embarrassing would that have been? Very.

When the Gorgon triplets reached the big bronze front doors of the Academy, each of them slipped off their regular sandals and grabbed a pair of silver-winged ones from the basket nearby. Then they went outside and down MOA's wide granite steps, where they sat and slipped the sandals on. Once the laces magically twined around their ankles, they stood.

Immediately the silver wings at the heels of her immortal sisters' sandals began to flap. Stheno and Euryale rose to hover a few inches above the tiled court-yard. But Medusa's sandaled feet remained firmly on the ground, wings unmoving. That is, until her sisters came to stand on either side of her and each took one of her hands in theirs.

At their immortal touch the wings on Medusa's sandals began to flutter too. "Whoa!" she said nervously as she rose to hover between them. She gripped their hands with her own white-knuckled ones. It didn't matter how many times she'd done this, it was still a frightening experience. Because her sisters controlled these sandals, not her! Only by clinging to an immortal's hand could a mortal fly.

"Let's go!" said Stheno. With that the three of them whisked away across the courtyard at ten times the speed of walking.

Medusa tightened her grip on Euryale's hand. "You're cutting off my circulation," Euryale complained. Medusa pretended not to hear. Back in third grade they'd once accidentally dropped her when they were first learning to use the sandals. She'd skinned her knees badly, and every time she looked at the scar on her left knee, she was reminded of how much she depended on them. It was awful to be so needy. Just one more reason she wanted to be a goddessgirl. Then she could take care of herself.

Minutes later they were inside the Immortal Marketplace, which was located halfway between the Academy and Earth. A magical talking wedding cake as tall as they were greeted them just inside the mall entrance. "Gods Gift is where you want to go if you're shopping for Zeus and Hera," it said, pointing them toward a store selling wedding gifts.

"I bet I won't be able to buy much with my eight drachmas," hinted Medusa as she and her sisters headed there together. "That's all I have saved." She hoped they would say they'd each loan her enough to get something really nice. But they didn't.

There was a scroll posted in the display window at Gods Gift. In swirly gold letters it announced:

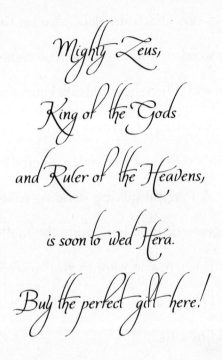

Mighty Zeus,

King of the Gods

and Ruler of the Heavens,

is soon to wed Hera.

Buy the perfect gift here!

Medusa headed inside, and her sisters followed. Every shelf and table in the store was covered with splendid wedding gifts set atop white satin tablecloths edged with real pearls. Artfully arranged among the gifts were decorations that included papyrus-tissue wedding bells and big white gift boxes with elaborate bows. She had a feeling the boxes were empty, because all the actual gifts were unwrapped and on display.

She actually did need to buy a gift for the wedding, she realized as she looked around. After all, everybody knew how much Principal Zeus liked presents.

Some of the gifts for sale were silly, like the pair of GodsBobble dolls. They were dressed as a bride and groom and stood about six inches high. *Those were probably Zeus's idea*, thought Medusa. She could just imagine them on top of his wedding cake, their heads constantly boinging up and down on springs every time his booming footsteps shook the ground. But the set of elegant silver goblets engraved with the entwined letters *Z* and *H* had to be Hera's idea.

Maybe if she found a gift that cost at least thirty drachmas, her sisters would lend her the twenty-two drachmas she needed. She could buy a gift here today, then return it tomorrow for a refund. With their drachmas plus her eight, she'd have the thirty she needed to buy the Immortalizer. She wouldn't *need* money once it turned her into a goddess. Because with her newfound immortal powers, she'd be able to *create* a superfabulous amazing wedding present. It was the perfect plan!

"Help me pick something out," she said, reaching up to nudge her snakes. Eager to oblige, they began flicking their tongues toward their choices.

"Are you talking to those slimy reptiles again?" Stheno asked.

"Reptiles aren't slimy," Medusa replied, setting aside the goblet she was holding. "Here, want to pet one and see for yourself?" She angled her head toward her sister.

"*Eek!*" Stheno jumped back. "Get those things away from me."

Medusa smiled. She'd thought having snakes for hair was going to be a curse at first. But in the months since Athena's Snakeypoo invention had accidentally turned her hair reptilian, these snakes had become her best buds. They were really rather sweet and fun. Like pets. And if someone messed with her, they stood up for her—or rather *lashed out*. She trusted them and could be herself around them. Something she couldn't do with anyone else.

"Can't you wear a hat or something?" complained Stheno, keeping her distance from Medusa.

"Yeah, those snakes are embarrassing. And they mock us," said Euryale.

"Huh?" said Medusa.

"Like that." Stheno pointed to a spot above Medusa's head.

Spying a delicate hand mirror—one of the gifts Hera had probably chosen—Medusa reached for it to check her reflection. Luckily she stopped herself just in time. Since she was mortal, she could turn herself to stone with one glance too! Instead she looked upward, smoothing her snakes down her forehead like bangs, to eye them better. They squirmed beneath her gaze, like they knew they'd been doing something they shouldn't have, the little rascals.

"They were making faces at us," Euryale told her, sounding annoyed. "Don't pretend you didn't know. They do it all the time."

Medusa grinned at her snakes, delighted. She actually hadn't known, but she thought it was funny. Giving them a wink, she let them loose, and they sprang upward again. Then she said to her sisters, "How would I know? Can you see the top of *your* head?"

"C'mon, Euryale. Let's go to Cleo's Cosmetics," Stheno suggested, sounding bored. "I need some more green face powder. And I want to hit that new store, The Green Scene. All their clothes are green. How cool is that?"

It sounded very cool to Medusa, but if they left, she wouldn't be able to carry out her plan. She tried to think of a way to stop them. They just *had* to give her a loan!

But her sisters were already pushing open the exit door. "Meet us back at the marketplace entrance in one hour," Stheno called over her shoulder. Both sisters gave her and her snakes the stink eye and then flounced off to shop on their own.

"Fine. Be that way," Medusa muttered. She'd just have to talk them into lending her some money later. The first step was to find a gift that cost thirty drachmas. And another that cost only eight. Then she'd show them how great the former was and how lame the latter was. Since they cared about appearances, surely they wouldn't want their sister to show up with the ickiest gift at the whole wedding. When they finally caved and gave her the loan, she could put her perfect plan into action. And the Immortalizer would be hers!

As she passed the GodsBobble dolls, she tapped their heads and watched them bounce. The she picked them up, looking for a price tag. Maybe these could be her eight-drachma gift. "Hmm. No price tag," she murmured.

"None of our gifts are marked. Please make an inquiry to me if you wish to know a price," said a stiff, formal voice.

Medusa glanced around in surprise. "Who said that?"

"I did." Then she noticed that the lid had lifted on the nearest decorative box, and a puppet had popped out like a jack-in-the-gift-box. It wore a white tunic with a formal black bow tie at its neck. There were similar gift boxes, each about ten inches square, sitting on every table. Did they all contain such helpful puppets?

"Okay. How much are these bouncy dolls?" she asked the puppet.

"I'm sorry, but those have already been purchased. You'll have to make a different choice." The puppet looked down its long nose at her. Medusa felt about the size of a green pea under its snooty gaze. And whenever anyone tried to make her feel small, she fought back!

"Fine. I will, Jack," she told him, mimicking his snooty tone.

"Why are you calling me Jack?"

"No reason, Jack," she said, smugly. She picked up an odd-looking shoulder bag that looked sort of like Artemis's arrow quiver. Only instead of olive wood this bag was made of gold! Scenes of Zeus's heroic exploits had been exquisitely carved on its surface.

"What's this?" she asked.

"An over-the-shoulder thunderbolt holder," the gift box replied.

Medusa giggled. This *had* to be Zeus's idea. "What does it do?"

In formal tones the gift box began describing it for her. "Made of the finest hammered gold from the mines of Thásos, the thunderbolt holder is four feet long and fifteen inches in diameter, with a woven filigree strap that is eight feet long. This magnificent item can contain the force and fury of three dynamic thunderbolts at any given time. It—"

The jack-in-the-gift-box droned on, but Medusa was thinking so hard now that its voice sounded far away. As she ran her hand over the gleaming gold of the thunderbolt holder, she remembered how Zeus had once granted Athena a single wish. It was earlier in the year, back when she'd invented the olive tree to win the school invention contest. Athena's wish had been for an old friend from Earth to visit her at MOA.

Medusa knew what she would have wished for—immortality! This golden thunderbolt holder was something special. If she gave it to Zeus, he would surely take notice and favor her. And he sometimes granted wishes to those he favored. Maybe this thing would do the trick. It *was* pretty amazing. You never knew with him.

"Is it sold?" she asked anxiously.

"No."

Relieved, she asked, "How much?"

"A mere three hundred drachmas."

"What?" Medusa's eyes went wide.

"Remember, it's pure gold from Thásos," the puppet informed her, beginning to go through his description all over again. Quickly she set the thunderbolt holder down, and the puppet stopped speaking midsentence.

Moving away, she began lifting other gifts on other

tables, one by one. Each time, the nearest gift box puppet popped up and gave her the price along with a description of the item.

"Oh, no!" she groaned after the twelfth Jack-puppet stated yet another price that was crazy expensive. Everything cost too much! There wasn't a single gift in here for thirty drachmas, much less eight. She couldn't even afford the cheapest gift—a silver thimble! So much for her perfect plan. Now what was she going to do? She couldn't be the only one at the wedding with no gift at all!

Dejected, she started out of the store. With each step she felt like she was dragging the weight of the world behind her—literally.

Screech! She winced. What was that noise? *Screech!* It sounded every time she took a step toward the shop's door.

As she was pushing the door open, a snooty voice shouted, "Stop, thief!" Medusa glanced back to see one of the jack-in-the-gift-box puppets staring in her direction and getting rather apoplectic.

She looked around. She was the only customer in the shop right now. "Who, me?" she asked, looking over at the puppet.

"Yes, you! Someone call the security guards!" yelled the Jack.

"What? Why? I'm not doing anything!"

But as she shoved the exit door wide, she heard that terrible screeching sound again. Something really *was* dragging behind her. Turning, she saw what it was. The golden thunderbolt holder!

She reached up and felt for her snakes. All twelve of them had wrapped themselves around the thunderbolt holder's carrier strap. They must've grabbed hold of it when she'd passed by the display table a minute before.

Her snakes were shoplifting!

4

Double-Dealing

DROP IT!" MEDUSA SCOLDED HER SNAKES.

"You're going to get us in trouble!" She shook her head

until they loosened their grasp on the carrier strap. *Bam!*

The thunderbolt holder hit the floor.

Medusa picked it up and set it on the nearest table.

"There. Problem solved," she told the blabby Jack. But it

was too late! By now all the other gift boxes in the store

had begun to chime in with calls of, "Thief!" "Halt!" "Security!" "Get her!"

The marketplace's security guards were going to be after her any minute, she thought wildly. Heart pounding, she did the only thing she could think to do. She ran.

Dashing from the store, Medusa darted around a corner, then ducked through a clothing store and out a side door. Finding herself in the marketplace atrium, she hunkered down next to the splashing fountain at its center. She curled into a ball under a rhododendron bush, hardly daring to breathe.

Heavy footsteps approached. *Thump! Thump!* Security guards hot on her trail, no doubt. Since she was green, she luckily blended in quite nicely with the plants surrounding the fountain. The guards ran past without noticing her!

She waited till their footsteps faded, wondering what

to do next. Should she turn herself in and explain the situation? No, it was too late for that. She would look guilty because she'd run.

Since she was the only person she knew with snake hair, it wasn't going to be hard for the guards to find her once the gift boxes ratted her out, though. Would this get her kicked out of MOA? School rules clearly stated that students would be expelled for stealing. Really, her snakes had done it. But who would believe she hadn't put them up to it?

Besides, if her snakes wound up having to go to reptile jail or something, she'd have to go too. They were attached to her head, after all. *Ye gods!* She had to get out of here before they were caught!

When the coast was clear, Medusa grabbed an empty flowerpot sitting nearby, turned it upside down, and set it atop her head. *My sisters would be pleased I'm wearing a hat,* she thought hysterically, *even if it is made of terra-cotta!*

Hoping the flowerpot hat would make her less recognizable, she slipped from the atrium garden. As she headed in the opposite direction of the footsteps, she made herself walk calmly so as not to draw unwanted attention. Once she reached the main exit doors, she set the pot down and darted outside.

How long till her sisters showed up to meet her? she wondered. Had it been an hour yet?

Suddenly she heard a shout. Two guards burst through the doors and came stomping outside. She had to get out of here! If only she had the magic to make her winged sandals fly. Honestly, being mortal really stunk sometimes!

She dashed around the nearest corner. Parked just ahead she saw a beautiful silver chariot with mighty white wings. It was mounded high with small papyrus tubes. Hermes' Delivery Service chariot! She rushed toward it and dove into the back.

The tubes were actually small scrolls, she discovered, each only about ten inches long. She dug her way through hundreds of them to hide underneath. Once she was completely covered up, she smoothed all twelve of her snakes back. Then she looped them in a ponytail at the base of her neck so they wouldn't pop up and give away her hiding place.

The guards thundered past, the sound of their footsteps eventually fading in the distance.

"That was a close call, guys," she quietly scolded her snakes. "I know you were just trying to help me out, but shoplifting could get us kicked out of the Academy.

Promise me you'll never, never, ever, ever try something so stupid again."

The snakes curled around her neck, their way of saying they were sorry. Since they usually napped in the middle of the day and were exhausted by all the excitement, they soon settled down to sleep. Medusa pushed a few scrolls aside and peeked from the back of the chariot. No guards in sight.

Still, this was a good hideout. She'd wait here until she was absolutely sure the coast was clear. And at the same time she'd keep an eye on the mall entrance to watch for her sisters.

One of the cream-colored scrolls poked her cheek, and she pushed it away. All the scrolls were identical, she realized, each one addressed in sparkly gold writing and tied with a gold ribbon. She managed to unroll one of them and read:

You are hereby invited to

the illustrious wedding

of the mighty

Zeus,

King of the Gods and Ruler of the Heavens

to

Hera,

soon to be Queen of the Gods and Co-Ruler of the Heavens.

Nuptials to take place

next Sunday at noon.

Don't even think about being late!

These were Zeus and Hera's wedding invitations!
When Medusa let go of the scroll, it magically rolled
back up with a *snap* and its ribbon retied itself. Hermes
must be planning to deliver the scrolls all over Mount

Olympus and Earth. She examined more of them. Some were addressed to dignitaries and officials, and others to the wedding couple's relatives and friends.

Hearing a soft flapping that grew increasingly louder, she cocked her head to listen. What was that sound? She puzzled over it for a minute, before it finally dawned on her. The chariot's wings!

Before she could climb out, the chariot gave a huge lurch. "Up and away!" called Hermes, causing the chariot to lift off the ground. *Whoosh!* In an instant they were zooming upward. Medusa slid sideways, then tumbled backward as they flew ever higher, sailing into the clouds.

"Wait!" she protested, but she was buried so deep in the scrolls by now that it sounded more like "mmpthf." It was no wonder Hermes didn't hear her. She tried to claw her way out of the scrolls, but it was like trying to make her way out of wedding invitation quicksand!

"Wait!" she shouted again when she was finally able to stick her head out.

The chariot wobbled horribly as hands reached back and grabbed her around the shoulders, pulling her out of the scrolls until she found herself face-to-face with a god wearing a winged cap. Sure enough, it was Hermes. And he did not look happy.

"Aha! I wondered why my chariot was riding rough," he told her. "Too much weight. You know what happens to stowaways, don't you?" Suddenly she found herself hanging in midair just outside the chariot, with the wind whipping her chiton, and nothing but clouds below her feet. Any minute now she feared he might shout "Medusa away!" and drop her. Then she and her snakes would be history.

"No! I didn't mean to stow away," Medusa protested.

"It was an accident! Take me back to the Immortal Marketplace, or better yet, to MOA. Please."

"Not gonna happen. I'm behind schedule already. My merchandise deliveries have been delayed until I can get all of Zeus's wedding invitations out." Hermes nodded toward the scrolls filling his chariot.

"I could help you with that," Medusa offered quickly. "I could drop off the invitations while you drive."

He wrinkled his brow, as if considering. "That *would* speed things up," he said at last.

"Yeah, and afterward you could drop me off at MOA in thanks, right?"

"Deal." Nodding, Hermes pulled her back inside.

Medusa spent the rest of the day flying across purple mountains and sparkling blue seas and tossing invitations here and there. Her snakes thought this was great fun, and turned out to be a big help in flinging the little scrolls into mailboxes.

By the time Hermes arrived on the coast of the Aegean Sea, at an open-air shopping market called an agora, Medusa was tired and hungry. So were her snakes.

"Why are we stopping here?" she asked, looking around. This was her hometown! Where she'd been born and lived until leaving for MOA. She hadn't been back since, and this was pretty much the last place on Earth she wanted to be. So Hermes' next words filled her with dread.

"Out you go," he said. "The rest of these invitations are bound for lands too magical for you to visit. No mortals allowed." He picked her up by the back of her chiton and set her on the ground.

She grabbed the side of the chariot and tried to

scramble back inside. "No! Wait. What about your promise to take me to Mount Olympus?"

Hermes gave her a cocky farewell salute. "I'll get you there as promised, but not until tomorrow."

"What am I supposed to do till then?"

He shrugged as he lifted off. "Your parents live here, don't they? Stay with them tonight and have a nice visit. But be back in this spot at nine sharp tomorrow morning when I swing by to pick you up on my way to MOA. If you're not here on time, I won't come looking for you."

As he lifted higher, Medusa jumped back to avoid being whomped by the enormous white wings on the chariot's sides, which had already begun to flap.

Watching Hermes sail away, she felt her heart sink. She did *not* want to be here.

Suddenly her stomach growled. Food vendors in the

nearby agora were baking, and the smell of warm bread filled the air around her. It was way past lunchtime, and her snakes were droopy. They were starving too. "C'mon, guys. Let's eat."

Quickly she reached into her pocket and slipped on the stoneglasses she always carried. Athena had invented these spectacles for mortals to wear in Medusa's presence, so they wouldn't be turned to stone. But Medusa had discovered that if she wore a pair herself her gaze wouldn't turn anyone to stone. Perhaps they would protect against her own reflection too, only she'd never been daring enough to peek into a mirror and find out!

Still, as she strolled through the agora, mortals ducked and ran for cover when they noticed her. Obviously they didn't trust her not to rip the glasses off and glare them into statues. Their fear was a little embarrassing. Maybe even hurtful. No, she was just weak from hunger—that would explain why she was feeling so weirdly vulnerable.

Smirking at those she passed, she pretended she was pleased to have inspired such alarm. And a small part of her *was* pleased. After all, turning mortals to stone was the closest thing to immortal magic that she could do!

The agora was every bit as noisy as she remembered. Merchants were selling products brought from trade ships—linen from Egypt, spices from India, and dates from Phoenicia. Criers called out special deals and sales. One vendor announced that fresh fish had just arrived from the boats docked in the harbor. Prices were never firm, and shoppers all around her haggled loudly with the merchants. The rich among them pulled their money from their purses, but poor shoppers carried their few coins in their mouths to keep them safe from thieves.

Even though Medusa was starving, her snakes' needs

came first. She bought some dried peas from a booth and began tossing them into the air as she browsed through the shops. Her snakes snapped at the snacks, gobbling them down hungrily. When the peas were gone, she turned to go down a different aisle. Hearing whispers, she looked over her shoulder and saw that a bunch of townspeople had been following her. They were fascinated by the sight of her feeding her snaky hair.

"Show's over!" she called. Making a scary face, she shooed everyone away. As she continued on through the agora, she noticed a crowd in one of the shops. The store was new since she'd last been here. The sign above its door read BE A HERO! Just then her stomach growled again. *Mmm. Hero sandwiches,* she thought.

But when she went inside, she discovered that it was a gift shop, not a restaurant. Still, the shop did sell *some* food, including hero sandwiches. She bought one to munch and noticed a familiar face on the sandwich packaging. It was that of Heracles—a mortal boy who also attended MOA. In fact, everything on the shelves in this shop bore the face, logo, or autograph of some mortal hero. Mostly they were Trojan War heroes. She saw Odysseus's likeness on a tunic and Paris's face on a heart-shaped box of candy.

"Welcome! It's Medusa, right? Your snakes are a dead giveaway," said a voice behind her.

"Wah?" Medusa replied around a mouthful of sandwich. Turning, she saw a short round man with slicked-back black hair and a dark mustache that formed huge stiff curls at either end. He bowed low, and she blinked in surprise. She'd never seen anyone wearing a bright yellow-and-black checkered tunic before.

"How *fabulous* that you've come to my shop! *Such* an honor!" As he spoke, he waved his arms, making grand sweeping gestures like a magician. "Ah, but you must allow me to introduce myself. Mr. Dolos, at your service." He bowed low again. "Now hurry, hurry. Come this way. There's no time to lose. Fame and fortune await!"

Medusa gulped her last bite of sandwich. She didn't care about fame, but the word "fortune" drew her like a fly to honey. Abandoning her usual caution, she followed him across the store, weaving through the crowd of customers. Going behind the checkout counter, he began digging around in a box of papers on a shelf.

"Ah, here we are!" He slid a scroll across the counter to her. The word "contract" was written at the top, but his hand was covering most of the other words on it. With his other hand he held out a feather quill pen. "Just sign on the dotted line, and fame and fortune are yours!"

Medusa hesitated. "How much fortune are we talking about?"

He reached down under the counter and brought out a bag that was heavy with coins. "Twenty drachmas." Her eyes widened, and he smiled, showing a row of shiny gold teeth. "And that's just for starters."

"What do I have to do?"

"Not a thing! By signing you agree to license your likeness. I'll take things from there. Just imagine! Products you've endorsed will be sold in this very shop right alongside those of the famous hero Odysseus!" He waved a gloved hand to indicate the displays around the store.

"You mean Odysseus and these mortal heroes licensed their likenesses for all the products you sell? Heracles, too?" Medusa found it hard to believe that Heracles would do that.

"But of course!"

He pushed the contract and pen closer to her, hinting.

She looked down at it. "Shouldn't I read it first?"

He twirled one end of his mustache between two fingers. "Ah! I can see you're a smart girl! But I assure you it's a simple, standard agreement. You license your image, and I sell products with it. Simple!" He winked.

Her snakes flicked their tongues at him, which meant they didn't trust him. Usually they were right about people, but she was blinded by the flash of gold and ignored their warning. "Calm down," she murmured to them. If Heracles had signed a contract, it must be on the up and up, right? So why shouldn't she sign too?

But still she hesitated. "All those other products have heroes on them. I'm no hero," she said.

"Ah, but I believe your image will make mortals *feel* like heroes!"

"Really?" Medusa couldn't help feeling flattered.

Mr. Dolos nodded, looking very sincere. He leaned in, whispering now. "Confidentially, I think products with your image will blow my customers out of their sandals. You'll be a bestseller!"

Remembering that everyone in the agora haggled, she said, "In that case I want *thirty* drachmas."

Without hesitation Mr. Dolos reached under the counter and set another slightly smaller bag of drachmas on the counter beside the first bag. "Here you go. This is just the down payment. Every time I sell your image, you'll earn more. It adds up, let me tell you. There's money to be made in licensing."

This guy was crazy to think people would buy products with her face on them. They *ran* from her face. But who cared! If he wanted to give her thirty drachmas for just signing her name, no way was she going to refuse. Dazzled by his persuasion and his gold, Medusa signed. Before the ink could even dry, he whisked the contract away, exclaiming, "Congratulations!"

A few minutes later she left the shop with thirty drachmas in her pockets and a smile on her face. Wow— what a great deal she'd just made!

"Hey, it's Gorgonzola!" she heard someone yell.

In an instant the smile left her face. Glancing over one shoulder, she saw a bunch of kids from her old school. Ugh. She hated that nickname. Gorgonzola was a kind of smelly cheese, and since her last name was Gorgon, kids had used it to tease her. No one had teased her immortal sisters, though, for fear of being smote into oblivion.

Well, now she had her own weapon—her stoneifying gaze. And she'd show them!

Heading straight for the group of kids, she reached

for the stoneglasses she wore, as if she planned to take them off. "Did I hear someone say they wanted to be turned into a marble statue?" she called out.

Shrieking, the kids ran off. Watching them, Medusa smirked and said to herself in a satisfied voice, "*Humph! I didn't think so.*"

5

Home Unsweet Home

I'M HOME!" MEDUSA ANNOUNCED AS SHE THREW open the front door of the cottage where she'd grown up as a little girl. Her mom looked up from the seaweed stew she was cooking. Medusa wrinkled her nose. She hated seaweed stew. MOA's ambrosia stew was much tastier.

Her mom, Ceto, looked over at her anxiously. "Dusa? Why are you home from school? What's wrong? Are your sisters okay?" She waddled closer. She couldn't help the way she walked; she was a sea monster, and all she could do was waddle or slither when she was on land. In the sea she could swim like a fish, though. Medusa and her sisters had inherited her swimming talent.

"Stheno and Euryale are fine," said Medusa, looking around. "I am too, if anyone cares," she added in a voice too soft for her mom to hear.

The house looked exactly the same as when she'd left it years ago to follow her sisters to MOA. She hadn't come back here since, not even on holidays. One entire wall of the kitchen was covered with swimming medals and academic awards her sisters had won over the years. None of Medusa's were on display, but she hadn't expected them to be. Her parents had never made any secret of liking her sisters better than her.

"Phorcys! Your youngest daughter has finally come

to visit," her mom shouted toward the living room. "What do you think of that?"

Reading a scrollazine in his favorite chair, her dad, Phorcys, just grunted without looking over. He was a sea hog, and that was pretty much the way sea hogs talked—in gruntspeak.

"What in the world have you done with your hair?" her mom demanded in horror, seeming to just now notice the snakes. "Is that some kind of fad? Regular hair isn't good enough for you now that you're going to school with immortals?"

"It was an accident," said Medusa as she went over to pour a drink from the water pitcher on the counter. "An invention mistake."

"Well, it looks ridiculous. I certainly hope you're not going to keep it that way."

Medusa shrugged and set her drink aside. She doubted her hair was going to change no matter what her mom hoped. Athena had told her there was no way of reversing the effects of Snakeypoo (which Athena had actually originally named Snarkypoo).

"So how's school?" her mom asked. "Have you finally come to your senses and realized you belong back here in Greece with other mortals? It's about time. I don't know why you had such foolish uppity ambitions in the first place. Like I always told you, no matter how much you study, you'll never be immortal."

"Thanks, Mom," Medusa said, rolling her eyes. "Nice of you to tell me something I don't already know."

But her mom didn't pick up on the sarcasm and just blabbered on. "Anyway, I'm glad you're here," she said.

Medusa's head jerked back in surprise. "You are?"

Her parents were always glad to see her sisters, but they didn't give a hoot about her. In fact, they hadn't sent her a single letterscroll the whole time she'd been at MOA.

"Yes, I've packed up all the old stuff you left in your room," her mom went on. "We plan to use your bedroom for storage. Since you're here, you can help me take the boxes down to donate to charity."

"You're ditching my stuff?" Alarmed, Medusa didn't wait for her mom to continue. Quickly she dashed from the kitchen through the living room to get to her bedroom. Along the way she passed dozens of framed sketches and paintings of her sisters. Some sat on the fireplace mantel, others on shelves or on side tables. But there were none of Medusa.

Her childhood bedroom was as small as a walk-in closet. Not surprising, since it actually had been a closet until she was born. There were no windows, so she lit a candle before going inside.

Sure enough, all of her stuff had been packed up into two boxes, which were sitting in the middle of her closet-room. Her bed, which had once filled most of the floor space, was already gone. Setting the candle in a holder, she kneeled and opened the first box. It was full of old clothes and sandals that didn't fit her anymore, so she closed it and opened the second one.

This one was full of treasures. There were old shells she'd collected, an ancient coin she had found washed up on the seashore, and a mermaid doll she'd made out of sticks and sea grass. There were hundreds of drawings she'd made in first and second grade, before she'd left home.

Medusa kept digging, searching until she found a particular set of scrolls. She unrolled them on the floor and studied one of the many *Queen of Mean* comic strips she'd drawn when she was little. She was the star of every comic. A superhero!

Her drawings were mostly stick figures with big O-shaped heads. But she'd added touches to the characters that had made them individuals. The comics were almost like a diary, because the drawings showed things that had happened to her during the years she'd lived at home.

Even with the candle she could barely see in her dark bedroom. Taking the whole set of comic-scrolls and the candle, she went across the hall to the room her sisters had shared. Not a thing had been changed in their room since they'd left home. Their frilly green bedspreads were freshly washed in case they dropped by to visit. Their books, toys, and dolls still sat on shelves that had been recently dusted.

Medusa walked over and flopped down right in the middle of one of those perfectly made beds. Lying on her stomach, she began reading the comics. Her snakes peered at them too, as if curious about her childhood.

As the Queen of Mean she had used something she'd called payback magic to get even with dastardly evildoers. (Evildoers were basically whoever treated her badly.) Her weapon was a magic cheese. When she held it high and yelled "gorgonzola," her enemies turned into cheese.

She wasn't sure why she'd chosen to have the queen-superhero shout that horrid nickname, since she hated it. Maybe it was because turning the name against her enemies had drained away some of its power to hurt her.

She laughed at the comic where she turned a kid into cheese for stealing her lunch money. And at the one where she turned her sisters into cheese for making her miss the end-of-the-year first-grade party. They'd ratted her out about her messy room, and her parents had insisted she stay home and clean it. The party, called the Fin-derella Ball, had been sea-themed. Her sisters had dressed up as twin sea nymphs. In her comic strip they'd turned into twin cheeses when the clock struck twelve.

"Ha-ha-ha!" She chuckled to herself. She'd been pretty hilarious as a little kid, even if she did say so herself. Before she could even write, she could draw pretty well. She'd forgotten that. Resting her chin on one hand, she kept reading, laughing softly. But after a while she started to yawn now and then too. Her head began to nod and her eyelids grew heavy.

Next thing she knew, her mom was screeching at her. "Dusa! What are you doing in here?"

"Huh?" Rubbing her eyes, Medusa sat up and looked around. It was morning, and she was lying on one of her sisters' beds. What was she doing back at home? Was this a dream—that is, a nightmare?

Then she remembered all that had gone on the day before. "What time is it?" Leaping from the bed, she checked the sundial outside and saw it was nearly nine o'clock. She was supposed to be meeting Hermes for a ride back to Mount Olympus!

In a flash Medusa scooped up her Queen of Mean comic-scrolls. Clutching them to her chest, she hurried off. "Bye, Mom!" But her mom was already busy smoothing out the wrinkles she'd made in her sister's bedspread and only gave her a casual wave. She didn't even ask where she was going or if she'd be back.

Her dad was sitting at the table having seaweed flakes for breakfast as she dashed past. "Bye, Dad!" she called to him, but he only grunted in reply.

Medusa was breathing hard by the time she reached the spot where Hermes had told her to wait. But there was no Hermes and no chariot. Oh, no! Was she too late? Had he already come and gone? She stared at the sky anxiously.

"Medusa Gorgon! Is that really you?"

Medusa slipped on her stoneglasses before looking around to see who'd spoken. It was a girl who had been in her second-grade class here at her old school. A pot of water was balanced atop her head, and she was holding its handle with one hand.

"I knew it!" the girl said in excitement. "I'm Echidne, remember?" She glanced at the snakes on Medusa's head. "So it's true about your hair."

Medusa looked upward, scanning the sky. Still no Hermes. She glanced at the girl again. She'd been pretty nice—nicer than most of the other kids, as Medusa recalled. "Yeah, it's true. Um, are you headed to school?"

Echidne laughed. "Girls can't attend school after second grade around here, remember? I'm training to be a water-carrier," she said proudly.

"Awesome," Medusa said unenthusiastically. This was just the kind of job she had wanted to escape by leaving home.

"Not as awesome as your life at Mount Olympus Academy, I bet. So, what's it like hanging out with goddessgirls like Aphrodite and Athena?" The girl sighed wistfully. "They must be so beautiful and smart, and, well, goddessy."

"Yeah, they are," said Medusa. "We hang out all the time. In fact, we're like this." She held up two fingers twined together. "I sit at their table in the cafeteria for lunch most of the time. With Persephone and Artemis, too."

Echidne's eyes widened. "Really? You are *so* lucky!"

Yes, she was lucky, thought Medusa. Lucky not to still live here. After spending years with immortals, life down on Earth was not for her. She would be bored out of her mind if she had to return to this town, where she couldn't even go to school.

Yesterday's worry returned to nag at her again. What if Zeus had found out about her snakes' shoplifting? He wouldn't throw her out of the Academy and send her back here, would he?

Medusa had never been happier to see the white-winged silver chariot appear in the sky. The minute Hermes swooped down, she dove into the back of his chariot. Waving good-bye to her childhood schoolmate, who was gazing at the chariot in awe, she called, "Sorry. Gotta go!" But she wasn't really sorry to leave at all.

6

Fin-tastic

ALTHOUGH HERMES HAD FINISHED DELIVER-
ing Zeus and Hera's wedding invitations yesterday, he
took Medusa on his regular mail rounds on the way
to Mount Olympus. She helped toss out packages and
letterscrolls—not to be nice, of course—just to hurry
things along. It was noon by the time they finally

approached MOA. She hadn't had any breakfast, and she was starving again.

As they broke through a puffy white cloud, the majestic Academy burst into view. It gleamed in the sunlight atop the highest mountain in Greece. Built of polished marble, the Academy was five stories tall and surrounded on all sides by dozens of Ionic columns. Low-relief friezes were sculpted just below its peaked rooftop. It was so beautiful that sometimes she could hardly believe she actually got to go to school here. She only hoped nothing happened to send her back home!

The chariot's mighty wings flapped more slowly as they circled the school. "Next stop: Mount Olympus Academy," rumbled Hermes. "Looks like . . . Zeu . . . making . . . announ . . ." The wind caught his words and blew them away so that Medusa didn't understand most of what he said.

But as they landed, she saw Principal Zeus standing in the MOA courtyard with a crowd around him. The school herald stood at his side, which meant that the principal was about to make an official announcement.

Stopping for maybe two seconds, Hermes tipped the chariot just enough for Medusa to either hop out or fall out. She hopped. By some miracle she managed to hold on to her comic-scrolls. "You're welcome!" she called as he took off without a word of thanks for the help she'd given him with his deliveries. He only waved merrily, not seeming to realize she was annoyed.

Hermes' winged chariot always attracted attention, and heads turned their way as he flapped off. Had anyone heard about the shoplifting incident? Medusa wondered. "Incident" was Aphrodite's word for any big trouble she accidently caused—like starting the Trojan War. Shoplifting wasn't quite that bad, but still.

Speaking of Aphrodite—she and her three best buds—Athena, Persephone, and Artemis—were standing together in the crowd around Zeus.

Medusa also saw Pheme, her former roommate and her only sort-of friend at school. As the goddessgirl of gossip, she would surely know if there were any shoplifting rumors circulating. Still clutching her comic-scrolls, Medusa walked over to her. "Heard any new rumors lately?" she asked by way of greeting.

Pheme's eyes were glued to Zeus as if terrified she might miss the start of his exciting news. "Shh," she said, but at the same time she shook her head no.

Relieved, Medusa turned her attention to the herald as he called for quiet, then began speaking. "Since the number seven brings good fortune, it is tradition for an immortal groom to choose seven groomsmen to be in his wedding. Today Principal Zeus, King of the Gods and

Ruler of the Heavens, has come before you to do just that. So without further ado, I give you . . . Principal Zeus!"

Ado? thought Medusa. Who used that word? No one except the pompous MOA herald, as far as she knew.

Everyone clapped as Zeus stepped up to address the crowd. Unrolling a papyrus scroll, he began to read from it, his voice booming out like the thunder he was so famous for. "My lucky seven groomsmen were chosen from among MOA students, based on their achievement in scholarship, artistry, strength, music, heroism, and other stuff. Congratulations to Apollo, Ares, Dionysus, Eros, Hades, Heracles, and Poseidon."

As cheers went up for the honored immortal and mortal boys, Medusa's green eyes fastened on Poseidon. Dressed in a turquoise tunic, he looked even cuter than usual!

"As is also tradition in immortal weddings," Zeus

93

went on, "these groomsmen will choose seven girls to be Hera's bridesmaids. So I hereby command each boy to hold a contest to select his partner from among MOA students and the daughters of honored guests visiting for the wedding."

Medusa's ears perked up. After years of crushing on Poseidon, this could be her big break. Whatever contest he decided on—she was going to win it!

His speech done, Zeus took off, and the students headed for the cafeteria. Some of the chosen grooms-men held quick, silly contests to choose bridesmaids right away as everyone walked along.

Ares went first. "The winner of my bridesmaid contest," he called out to the crowd, "will be the first god-dessgirl I spy who has nine letters in her name, which must start with an *A* and end with an *E*." He glanced over at Aphrodite, whose hand he was holding, and said,

"We have a winner!" She smiled, which made her look even more beautiful, if that were even possible. *As usual,* thought Medusa. *Aphrodite's beauty and immortality ensured that everything worked out for her. Grrr. No fair!*

Heracles went next. "I will choose the first girl who can come up with the longest and shortest words ever written." There was a minute of dead silence as everyone tried to figure out the two words. This riddle was almost as good as those the Python had asked him in the Olympic Games!

Athena answered on the spot, of course. "Longest is 'pneumonoultramicroscopicsilicovolcanoconiosis,' also known as pneumonia. As for the shortest, well, there are some single-letter words, such as 'I.' But since that's not a word when written in lowercase, I say that the truly *shortest* word must be the lowercase *short* vowel 'a.'"

When Heracles declared her the winner, she looked delighted. And relieved. It was a no-brainer that she would want to be a bridesmaid in her own dad's wedding! You'd think Zeus would've realized that. Was it possible he was as clueless as her own dad? Medusa wondered. At least Zeus didn't speak in grunts, though.

Hades held his contest next, asking a question about the flowers in the Underworld. It was a question that only Persephone could possibly know the answer to. Naturally she won, but Medusa wasn't really paying attention. She was busy keeping Poseidon in her sights. When he announced his contest, she would pounce. And she would win!

A vision danced in her head, of herself as a bridesmaid holding a pretty bouquet of flowers as she walked at his side in next weekend's wedding procession. By the time they all reached the cafeteria, only four godboys—

Apollo, Dionysus, Eros, and Poseidon—had yet to declare a contest and so were still without partners.

In the lunch line, however, Apollo borrowed a helmet-shaped bowl from one of the lunch ladies. "If you want to partner me in the wedding, put your name in this bowl!" he called out as everyone began getting their lunches.

Figuring Poseidon probably wouldn't announce his contest till Apollo's was decided, Medusa zipped up to her room and stashed her comic-scrolls and the coin bags from Mr. Dolos in her closet.

When she returned to the cafeteria a few minutes later, Apollo's contest was still in progress. The helmet-bowl was still being passed from table to table as she sat to eat with her sisters. When it came into her hands, she saw Ares say something to Apollo and gesture toward her. Apollo glanced at her, alarmed. She grinned evilly, sure he was worried he might get her as his bridesmaid. Should she put her name in just for fun? No, she didn't want to take a chance he might draw it out. So she wrote Ares's name instead, thinking it would be funny if Apollo picked a boy's name. Ha-ha-ha!

Apollo's helmet-bowl finally made its way back to him after passing through every girl's hands. Holding it, he stood and made a show of closing his eyes and digging deep into the slips of papyrus. He pulled one out and read the name on it: "Cassandra!"

A girl with long, wavy fire-gold hair stood. "I had a feeling you'd choose me!" she called to him, laughing.

"Yeah, right," muttered Medusa. She didn't believe the girl for a minute, and it wouldn't surprise her if no one else did either. "Who's she?" she asked. Murmurs spread through the cafeteria as everyone else wondered about her too.

Within moments Pheme flitted up to the green triplets' table. "She's rumored to be the daughter of one of the kings visiting here for the wedding," she told them breathlessly. Then she dashed off to another table to spread the information before anyone else could. Recalling the hundreds of invitations she'd helped Hermes deliver, Medusa knew that lots of dignitaries and their families had been invited to MOA for the week's celebrations and marriage ceremony.

After lunch Eros took the helmet-bowl and invited all the girls who were interested in being his bridesmaid to follow him to the shooting range on the sports field. The cafeteria cleared out as everyone headed there to see what would happen. Once they'd all gathered, he asked the girls to pull their names from Apollo's helmet and tack them to a target he'd set up. When all was ready, Eros took aim and shot his arrow of love from fifty paces.

"Pheme!" he announced, reading the slip his arrow had pierced. When Pheme squealed with joy, a puff of smoke escaped her lips and formed a cloud heart above her head.

Now it was down to just Dionysus and Poseidon. Since Medusa's attention was on Poseidon, she hardly noticed when Dionysus announced his contest and put on his Love-Is-Blind blindfold—the same one he'd worn when he'd danced with her during Hero Week.

After Apollo spun him around a few times, Dionysus blindly headed for the nearest girl. And that happened to be Medusa! *Ye gods*—not again! She leaped out of his way, and he wound up tagging a mortal girl standing behind her.

"Her name is Ariadne. She's the daughter of King Minos from Crete," Medusa heard Pheme telling everyone. Ariadne looked thrilled to have been chosen.

100

Medusa felt a tiny spurt of regret but then dismissed it. She had her heart set on Poseidon!

All eyes turned to him now that he was the only groomsman left without a bridesmaid. Medusa held her breath as he finally made his announcement. "Since I'm godboy of the sea, I will hold a swimming contest next Saturday in the gymnasium pool. The winner will have the honor of partnering me in Principal Zeus's wedding on Sunday."

A swimming contest? How fin-tastic—um, fantastic! thought Medusa. Living on the coast of the Aegean Sea with a sea monster and a sea hog for parents, she had learned to swim almost before she could walk. She had a real chance at winning this one!

From the corner of her eye she peeked over at Pandora, who looked dismayed. They'd been in Gym-ology together last year, so Medusa knew the girl wasn't much of a swimmer. If Poseidon had wanted Pandora to win, he would've picked a contest that was easy for her, right? Maybe something like Twenty Questions. The fact that he hadn't must mean he wasn't crushing on her, after all.

"Follow me if you want to sign up for my contest," Poseidon called out. Feeling excited, Medusa joined the crowd of girls who trailed after him as he left the archery range. The girls lined up as he posted a sign-up sheet on the gym's notice board. He didn't stick around, though. Ares and some other godboys had called him over for a game of discus-throwing on one of the sports fields outside.

Even though she wanted to knock all the other girls out of the way and sign her name first, Medusa hung back. Only when the last girl had gone and the coast was clear did she approach the notice board. Frowning, she surveyed the names of her competition. She could easily beat the mortals. But many of the signers were immortals with magical powers. What chance did a mortal like her have against girls who could use magic in a race? The only way she'd stand a chance was if she were immortal herself! *Hmm.*

After quickly signing her name, she dashed back up to her dorm room. She grabbed the partially completed Immortalizer ad form from her desk and finished filling it out. Then she got the money bags from her closet. She poured all thirty drachmas Mr. Dolos had given her into one sack, tucked the form inside, and tied it closed. Finally she wrote the delivery address on the outside of the sack and set it on her windowsill.

Hesitating, she stared at the bag for a minute. What if she was making a mistake? Her mind told her there was no way the necklace would work. But her heart longed to become immortal. She decided to ignore reason. Her perfect plan just had to work!

Within minutes a magic breeze came along. The four winds and their breezes delivered much of MOA's mail. But when this breeze tried to lift the bag and couldn't, it called for backup:

It's too heavy for a single breeze.

Winds of strength, come help me, please!

As the breeze's words died away, a much stronger gust of wind arrived to join it. Easily lifting her bag together, they whooshed it away.

Medusa flopped onto her bed feeling hopeful and excited. Turning onto her side, she leaned on an elbow and rested her chin in one palm, gazing at her Poseidon bulletin board. Just imagine—by next week her brides-maid bouquet might be tacked up there. And there might be a picture of the entire wedding party too. One in which she was all dressed up, and with her hand on Poseidon's arm!

Pictures of Zeus and Hera's wedding would almost certainly appear everywhere. Including on the front page of *Teen Scrollazine* and in the *Greekly Weekly News*. Even her parents would have to be proud to see her as a bridesmaid in a wedding for the King of the Gods! They'd probably hang that picture up in their house. And even better, all the kids who'd been mean to her growing up would see it and know she'd truly made it at MOA!

A sudden creative urge to draw came over her. She pulled out the comic-scrolls she'd stowed in her closet. Once she found a scroll that was still mostly blank, she put pen to papyrus:

The Queen of Mean (episode # 24)
Best Bridesmaid Ever!

"In today's episode," she murmured, quickly sketching an evil-looking snake holding its tail in its mouth, "the dastardly villainous serpent Ouroboros comes along trying to ruin Zeus's wedding." Now she drew two stick-figure people keeling over from fright. "Zeus and Hera faint in terror at the sight of the serpent," she continued. "Everyone else hides, including all the godboys. Springing into action, the Queen of Mean summons payback magic by shouting, 'Gorgonzola!'"

As Medusa sketched a stick figure of the Queen of Mean holding a stinky cheese in one hand and some flowers in her other, she said: "In a flash the queen tosses her bridesmaid bouquet to Poseidon to hold for her and zooms to Zeus's rescue! Caught in the jaws of the giant serpent—who took its own tail out of its mouth long enough to latch on to him—the principal is terrified." With rapid strokes she drew a bug-eyed, scared-looking Zeus.

Then she drew four goddessgirls, all joined at the hip like a garland of cutout paper dolls. Underneath them she made a long, wavy line of water. "Just then, Athena, Aphrodite, Persephone, and Artemis trip and fall into the pool, making a mess out of their chitons and hair. '*Help us!*' they shriek. '*Aghhh!*'" Medusa grinned as she drew their wild-eyed faces, straggly hair, and dripping gowns.

As she wrote and drew, she snacked on dried ambrosia curls. Now and then she tossed a handful high, and her snakes playfully snatched at them, then gulped them down.

Eventually her tale wound to a close. "At last! The Queen of Mean defeats evil and banishes the serpent.

Zeus is so grateful that he promises to magically turn her into the goddess of . . ." Unsure what to write, she continued, "Of whatever she wants to be goddess of."

"Then Poseidon returns her bouquet and says, 'With your stony, superlative gaze and magic cheese, you always manage to save the day. You are awesome, Queen of Mean!'

"Then the four most popular goddessgirls at MOA give her a necklace with a golden GG charm that matches their own, and beg her to be their friend. She humbly agrees and becomes instantly popular too. The end."

Rereading her comic, Medusa giggled. It was a masterpiece!

7

Kindergarten Buddies

DETERMINED TO WIN POSEIDON'S CONTEST, Medusa dragged herself out of bed at six on Monday morning to practice her swimming. She stretched and yawned, tired from getting up so early, and from staying up late the night before to draw her comic adventures. After she dressed, she jogged across the courtyard and over to the gym, which housed MOA's swimming pool in its basement grotto.

She took the limestone stairs down to the pool below the gym floor, then shucked her chiton to reveal the swimsuit she wore underneath. As god of the seas Poseidon had created this underground pool. Only he could instruct it to form different shapes that would meet the needs of any race or event. He could add waterfalls, rocks, and various fishy creatures too. But for now the pool was a simple long rectangle. Braided sea grass ropes marked off the swim lanes.

Hearing splashing sounds, Medusa looked around in surprise. A dozen other girls—both mortals and goddessgirls—were already swimming laps. She'd expected the pool to be empty at this hour, but it seemed that others were just as determined as she was to be Poseidon's bridesmaid.

"Sorry, guys. I've got a lot of training to cram into six days," she told her sleepy snakes as she dove into the chilly water. She swam twenty lengths of the pool and, though pleased with her speed, was so tired afterward that she felt like wilted seaweed.

After swimming, the other girls had to spend time fixing their hair in the changing rooms. That was one of the great things about having snake hair, thought Medusa as she quickly got dressed. No primping needed. It always looked good!

On her way from the pool to class, she saw dozens of unfamiliar chariots parked on the gym side of the court-yard. She guessed they must belong to the guests who'd been arriving for the wedding ever since Saturday.

Hearing sharp words, Medusa turned to glimpse Zeus and Hera walking among the olive trees in the grove on the far side of the courtyard. They were deep in conversation and seemed unaware that Athena and Aphrodite were standing just outside the grove. Whenever other students passed by, the two goddessgirls acted like they were reading a textscroll they held between them. But this was only to hide what they were really doing—eavesdropping.

Suddenly Hera stopped cold and folded her arms in a way that showed she was mad. Was the happy couple arguing? *How intriguing.* Although Medusa didn't spread gossip like Pheme, she loved knowing people's secrets. Sometimes she could use them to her advantage.

Trying to act casual, she slowly swerved between students who were walking to and fro, and headed for the grove. Pausing to one side of the two goddessgirls, she bent down behind a potted lemon tree and pretended to tie her sandal. The goddessgirls were so busy listening in that they didn't even notice her.

"And why shouldn't I continue working at my wedding shop?" Medusa heard Hera ask.

"How will it look?" Zeus roared. "I don't want kings and heads of state, or my friends, to think I'm so poor that my wife has to work. Besides, I want all of your attention, sugarplum."

"Don't 'sugarplum' me," Hera said sharply. "I enjoy my job, and I plan to keep it after we marry. And that's that." She stalked from the grove. Zeus followed, hot on her heels, still arguing. Aphrodite and Athena shrank back, obviously hoping that Zeus wouldn't see them and realize they'd been spying. Luckily for them, he didn't.

"I wish she'd just quit her job," Athena murmured when they'd gone.

"No way You know your dad wouldn't be happy with a wife who didn't have her own interests," Aphrodite insisted. "He just needs time to realize that. Remember his answers to my quiz?"

"What quiz?" Medusa asked, popping up from her hiding place.

The two goddessgirls looked her way in surprise. Then Athena pointed an accusing finger at her. "This is your fault."

Medusa stiffened. "Me? What did *I* do?"

"You asked those questions at the Job-ology talk on Friday, that's what. The ones about why goddesses bother to have careers," said Athena. "If not for you, my dad wouldn't have cared two figs about Hera continuing to work after they marry."

"Right," Aphrodite agreed. "And after all the trouble we took to find Hera for him—"

Medusa snapped her fingers. "Aha! I get it. You set Zeus up with Hera on purpose, didn't you?"

"Yes, so don't mess things up," said Aphrodite. "It wasn't easy getting him to fill out my Lonely Hearts quiz so we could decide who to match him with. Athena had to slip it into one of his scrollazines so he'd see it and—"

"So you tricked Zeus into answering a quiz?" Medusa interrupted. Tapping her chin with a fingertip, she smirked at them. "Interesting. I wonder what he would do if he knew." With that she turned and headed for the school steps.

Athena and Aphrodite exchanged a look of alarm, then caught up with her. "We were only trying to find a companion who suited him," said Aphrodite.

"He was so miserable after my mom left. Remember?" added Athena.

Athena's mom was named Metis, and she was a real, actual fly that had lived inside Zeus's head. After she'd buzzed off to find a new life some time ago, Hera and

Zeus had gotten together at a school dance. It was apparent to Medusa now that Hera's presence at the dance had been no mere accident. Reluctantly, she had to admit that Aphrodite's matchmaking in this instance had been a success. When Zeus had been unhappy in his pre-Hera era, there'd been constant thunderstorms. Since he'd met Hera, the principal was all sunny smiles.

"You wouldn't try to ruin things by telling him what we did, would you?" Athena asked anxiously. "Because if you cause trouble and my dad winds up unhappy again, you'll be the most unpopular girl at school, and . . ." Her words drifted off as she seemed to suddenly recall that Medusa already *was* the most unpopular girl at school. "I mean—"

Athena's words stung, even if they were true. "Don't worry," Medusa said crisply. "Your secret is safe with me."

Moving ahead, she started up the steps to the Academy's front doors, but then called back over her shoulder, "For now, anyway!"

Smiling at having gotten the last word, Medusa raced up the rest of the steps. She burst through the bronze doors and then walked down the hall toward her first-period Hero-ology class.

Stirring up trouble didn't exactly make her happy, but it did give her a feeling of power. And being a mortal, this wasn't a feeling she got to enjoy very often. Besides, she still hadn't forgiven Aphrodite for tricking Dionysus into dancing with her that night during Hero Week.

Medusa was jolted back to the present when Artemis's dogs raced in front of her. She had to stop short to avoid a collision. *Grrr.* Those dogs were a menace, the way they were always dodging around students in the hallways.

If she wouldn't get in trouble for it, she'd sure like to turn *them* to stone. But she'd done that once before, and Athena had just changed them back.

Nearing the Hero-ology classroom, she found herself walking right behind Apollo and Dionysus. Immediately her mind returned to the Hero Week dance. She'd figured Dionysus was playing a joke on her that night, so she'd turned the tables and deserted him in the middle of their second dance.

She'd hoped he would be embarrassed when he discovered he was out there dancing alone. However, two other girls had quickly joined him after she'd left, foiling her attempt at revenge. And when he'd finally whipped off his blindfold, *they* were who he'd seen. Now she wasn't sure if he even knew he'd been dancing with her earlier. But maybe someone had told him afterward. It would explain why he'd been staring at her so much lately.

"You know Ariadne, that girl I chose for my brides-maid?" Dionysus said to Apollo as they walked ahead of Medusa. "Her family had to return home. Some problem with their pet Minotaur going on a rampage."

"Whoa! Guess you better look for a new bridesmaid," Apollo told him as they split up. "Later."

Apollo headed a few doors down to Philosoph-ology. Dionysus went into Hero-ology, and Medusa followed. The two of them walked around the edge of the giant game board table on one side of the room. It was a three-dimensional map with roads, valleys, villages, and castles. Small hero statues acted as game pieces, and real-life little scaly beasts peeked from the map's seas and oceans.

As they always did when they passed by, her snakes hissed at the sea snakes in the miniature Mediterranean Sea. Overhearing, Dionysus smiled back at Medusa. He had really cute dimples when he did that, she noticed.

"So I'm guessing hair sssnakes and sea sssnakes are ene-miesss?" he quipped.

Was he making fun of her snakes? Unsure, she ignored him and continued on to her desk.

After she sat down, she immediately began orga-nizing her stuff. Glittery green nail polish went on one corner of her desk. (She usually painted her nails during class while using Athena, whose desk was in front of hers, as a shield to hide from the teacher.) Her notescroll went in the center of her desk, and her feather pen beside it. Setting her bag on the floor, she then glanced up to find Dionysus standing there, staring at her.

"What?" she demanded, frowning.

He laughed. "Hey, don't look so excited to see me!"

"Do you want something?" she asked. Tapping her fingernails on the desktop in irritation, she braced for a crack about her snakes or herself. Why couldn't he just leave her alone?

Looking suddenly shy, and maybe a bit nervous, too, Dionysus shifted from one foot to the other. The most famous actor at the Academy—shy? That didn't make sense. He was the star of every play in Drama-ology and was used to being the center of attention. She stared into his purple eyes and was startled to see his cheeks flush.

"Well, I was just wondering if you might . . ." He shoved his hands deep into the pockets of his tunic. But before he could finish delivering whatever joke or insult he must've had in mind, Aphrodite and Athena appeared, taking the seats in front of her and across the aisle. "Uh. Never mind," he told Medusa. After saying hi to the two goddessgirls, Dionysus ambled off to his own seat with his usual happy-go-lucky smile back in place.

"Attention, class!" Hearing the teacher's voice, Medusa looked over to see Mr. Cyclops holding up a listscroll at the front of the room. "As you know, many dignitaries, immortals, kings, and heroes from other realms are visiting MOA this week to await Sunday's big wedding. Many have brought their families, including some preschool-age children.

So in the interest of strengthening our relations with other cultures, you have each been paired with a kindergarten buddy. Your assigned buddy will be your responsibility during my class all this week. Starting today."

Realizing that this probably meant no regular class assignments or homework that week as well, a cheer went up among the students. Mr. Cyclops smiled slightly. "As you've evidently guessed, our usual class activities will be suspended until next Monday."

Striking a dramatic pose, Dionysus clasped his hands

over his heart and let out a deep sigh. "My heart is breaking," he joked. "So, no test tomorrow?"

"Right. I know it's a huge letdown, but try to bear up," Mr. Cyclops replied, the single big eye in the middle of his forehead twinkling. Then he looked toward the door, which had just opened. "Ah! Come in, Ms. Hydra," he said. "And bring your charges. Welcome, children!"

Ms. Hydra slithered in, her nine heads bobbing and weaving as she herded the energetic five-year-olds into the room. Once they were all inside, she bade a relieved farewell and slithered away again, shutting the door behind her. Without her many-headed supervision, the kindergarteners began running wild in the classroom. They examined everything, crawling under desks, and tripping over the older students' feet.

Some of these kids were mortal. *Hmm.* For a split second Medusa imagined curbing the wildness in the room by turning them to stone. Would anyone really blame her? Reluctantly, however, she slipped on her stoneglasses and gazed warily at the newcomers. Who wanted a kindergarten buddy? Not her.

"Oh, aren't they adorable?" she heard Aphrodite coo. Athena nodded, like one of the GodsBobble dolls she'd seen at Gods Gift. Medusa rolled her eyes.

Mr. Cyclops began calling off sets of names from his list. Poseidon got a sea monster's son named Cetus as his kindergarten buddy. Dionysus got Perseus, a mortal boy whose parents owned the Perseus Shield Market on Earth. And Pheme got a mortal girl. Aphrodite and Athena seemed thrilled with their cute curly-haired buddies, two sea nymphs named Thetis and Amphitrite.

By the time Mr. Cyclops got to Medusa, all the other students had been matched with a buddy. There was only one little girl left. Her dark eyes sparkled and her black hair had been divided into dozens of braids, each one tied with a ribbon. "This is Andromeda, a princess from Ethiopia," Mr. Cyclops told Medusa. "She'll be your buddy."

The little girl took one look at Medusa and then burst into tears. "You can't make me go with her!" she shouted. Then she dashed into the supply closet and slammed the door shut behind her. Everyone turned to stare at Medusa, as if this were all her fault. Most kids were leery of her snakes.

Most grown-ups too. Oh, well. It was no skin off her green nose if she didn't have a buddy. For all she cared, the little girl could just stay in the closet! But then she felt Poseidon's eyes on her, waiting to see what she would do.

Not wanting to risk his disapproval, she sighed. "I'll get her." As she walked over to the closet, the rest of the class returned their attention to their own kindergarteners.

Some picked up books to read together; others got out games or art stuff.

Medusa opened the closet door and peeked inside. The little girl was curled up in a corner sucking her thumb. Using her friendliest voice, Medusa said, "Come on, don't be scared, Andromeda. My snakes won't hurt you."

The thumb popped out. "I'm not ascareduhsnakes. Unless they bite. Do they bite? Does it hurt to have them? Can they talk?" This kid asked as many questions as Pandora!

"Um, no," Medusa replied, answering all three questions at once.

The girl scooted forward, walking on her knees. "Can I pet 'em, then?" Standing, she reached out.

Medusa recoiled. No one had ever dared touch her snakes. Except Heracles, who'd tried to strangle them once—the jerk. Her snakes froze, unsure how to react either.

The girl put her hands on her hips, acting tough, but also looking a little hurt at Medusa's hesitation. "Okay. I guess. If you really want to," she told Andromeda at last. She kneeled down and bent her head.

Despite their initial uncertainty, the snakes seemed to take to the girl. Some wound around her wrist like bracelets, others gently flicked their tongues out to tickle her cheek. Andromeda giggled. A good sign. "Do they have names?" she asked, petting them.

No one had ever asked her *that* before either! "Yeah," said Medusa, beginning to feel flattered by Andromeda's interest. She pointed to each snake in turn, introducing them. "They're names are Viper, Flicka, Pretzel, Snapper, Twister, Slinky, Lasso, Slither, Scaly, Emerald, Sweetpea, and Wiggle."

After the girl had satisfied her curiosity and petted each snake, Medusa stood, trying to think up a way to get her out of the closet. "I don't think my snakes like it in here. So could you maybe come out? We could join your friends and you could teach them the names of my snakes." It would be something to do, at least. She'd never had a kindergarten buddy before. How was *she* supposed to know what to do with one?

"Don't have any friends. I'm new," Andromeda informed her.

"New at your school, you mean?"

Andromeda nodded. Taking Medusa's hand, she allowed herself to be led into the classroom. Medusa immediately noticed there was an empty spot between Poseidon and Heracles at the Hero-ology game board. What luck! She steered her buddy in that direction.

"Make way! For I am the brave-hearted Perseus!" a

boyish voice piped up. Medusa and Andromeda both jumped out of the way of the shaggy-haired little boy. He was riding on Dionysus's back, his legs looped around the godboy's waist as Dionysus pretended to gallop around.

"And I'm his winged sea horse," Dionysus informed them, his purple eyes twinkling. "We are riding the wild waves of stormy seas in search of a dangerous mission. And it looks like we found one, right, Perseus? Two princesses in need of rescue!"

Andromeda's eyes got big, and she squealed so loud that Medusa winced. "Princess Rescue is my favorite game *ever*!"

Dionysus sure was good with kids, Medusa thought. And he was right that she'd needed rescue—from not knowing what to do with her buddy! Within minutes she was following Andromeda's lead, pretending to be locked in a tower that stood upon an island in the middle of the sea.

"Oh, no! Waves are crashing all around us," Andromeda said in an excited voice, her imagination running wild. "And look! A scary serpent is swimming our way!" She pointed to Poseidon's sea monster buddy, Cetus, who had left the game board to come join in their game instead. Poseidon was right behind him.

Yes! thought Medusa, carefully acting un-thrilled about her crush's arrival.

"How will we ever escape?" Andromeda asked in pretend alarm, still focused on their game.

"We'll save you, won't we?" Perseus asked Dionysus as they galloped to their rescue.

"You bet, partner!" Dionysus assured him. He was taking all kinds of detours, trying to make the trip to reach them seem long and treacherous, which Perseus loved.

"Or maybe we could figure out a way to save our-selves," Medusa suggested to Andromeda.

"No! That's not how it works," Andromeda said, insisting that they wait for the boys to help them. Leaning back, she looked up and yelled to Medusa's snakes. "Come on, snakeys. Help us get them over here before we are chomped to smithereens!"

Medusa felt her snakes wiggling around, and figured they must be making directional signals. Diony-sus pretended to misunderstand, making hilarious wrong guesses about what the snakes were trying to tell him, which made Andromeda giggle.

Even though it was dumb, Medusa did think this game was kind of fun. But then, how could you not have fun with Dionysus around?

"You're a real snake charmer," Poseidon said, wink-ing at Andromeda. His sea monster buddy was now making growly noises and trying to look dangerous as he "swam" around the girls.

"I'm not a snake charmer. I'm a princess," Andromeda informed him. "The prettiest princess in the whole sea!"

Poseidon's eyes narrowed, and he frowned. "Oh, is that so? Because I'm the god of the sea, and—"

"You're a big fat liar," Cetus butted in, glaring at the little girl. Across the room Aphrodite and Athena's sea nymph buddies scowled and nodded in agreement.

Uh-oh. It was never a good idea to announce that you were beautiful around immortals or fantastic beasts. Someone always took offense and wanted to argue about it.

"It's true!" Andromeda insisted, glaring at Cetus. "My mom says I'm so pretty I could be in Hera's wedding."

Now Dionysus's little buddy spoke up. "I think so too," said Perseus.

Medusa looked at Andromeda, and felt a sudden urge to protect her. She couldn't let her get her hopes up. They'd only be dashed later on. "There's no way you'll be chosen for the wedding party," she explained bluntly. "For one thing you're a mere mortal. And your family has no connection to Hera or Zeus."

Andromeda stared at her, looking wounded. Then, for the second time that morning, her face crumpled into tears. "Meanie!" she wailed.

Aphrodite and Athena, who were now playing a Go Fish card game with their sea nymph buddies, looked over at Medusa, aghast. Others turned her way too, including the gossipy Pheme. And Mr. Cyclops. Medusa didn't get it. What was so mean about telling the truth?

Clumsily she patted Andromeda's head, trying to pretend all was well. But the girl only ducked away from her and cried harder still. Though Medusa felt bad

133

about upsetting her, she wasn't about to admit it. Not with everyone watching!

Before Mr. Cyclops got involved, Dionysus spoke up, "Hey, buddy," he said to Perseus. "Why don't you take Andromeda over to look at the hero game board?" When the two kids were gone, he drew Medusa aside. Keeping his voice low, he said, "What is wrong with you? Why do you always attack people like that?"

"You know she doesn't stand a chance of being in Zeus's wedding," Medusa protested. Why was he scolding her? It wasn't fair!

"She's a little kid!" Dionysus said, nodding toward Andromeda. "What's wrong with letting her enjoy her dreams?"

"What's *wrong* is that those dreams are totally unrealistic," said Medusa, putting her hands on her

134

hips in annoyance. "I'm only trying to save her from disappointment."

Dionysus shot her a look of disbelief. "So instead you crush her dreams? Nice going."

Leaving her, he went over to Andromeda. "Guess what?" he told her. "I'm going to be in the wedding on Sunday."

"You are?" Her tears slowed and she gazed at him in awe, as if she thought him the luckiest godboy ever.

He nodded. "And I get to choose any girl on Olympus or Earth that I want to walk down the aisle with me." Bowing, he said in a formal tone, "Princess Andromeda, will you do me the honor of being my bridesmaid?"

Andromeda's face lit up with a huge sunny grin. "Really?" At Dionysus's nod her smile widened even more and she curtsied prettily. "Yes, kind sir." Then she began twirling around with glee, chanting, "I'm gonna be in the wedding; I'm gonna be in the wedding!"

Suddenly Medusa felt a little greener than usual. Green with envy, that is. Almost as if she wished he'd asked *her* instead. But that was crazy! She couldn't be jealous of a five-year-old. Besides, it was Poseidon she liked, *not* Dionysus.

Why was Dionysus so critical of her, anyway? With everyone else he was always joking around. A lump formed in her throat. It must mean he really disliked her. She blinked back a few tears. *Well, so what?* she thought the very next minute.

Ping, ping, ping! Almost as if it knew how much she wanted to escape, the lyrebell rang right then. Pretending nothing was wrong, Medusa grabbed her stuff and marched out of the room with her head held high.

8
The Gray Ladies

PERSEPHONE'S MOM'S FLOWER SHOP IS DOING all the flowers for the wedding," Pheme told Medusa that afternoon as they sat together in the cafeteria. "And they've decided that the bridesmaids will wear orange roses." As usual, her words drifted above her head in little cloud letters. "That's going to look great with my orange lip gloss, don't you think?"

"Um-hmm," said Medusa. Taking a bite of ambrosia salad, she watched Poseidon out of the corner of her eye. He, Apollo, and Ares were each trying to balance their empty nectar cartons on one fingertip as they headed for the tray return.

"And Hera will be carrying a big bouquet of them, so we'll all match. Doesn't that sound awesome?"

"Um-hmm," said Medusa, sipping her nectar. Because Pheme had been talking nonstop, she hadn't eaten a single bite of her nectaroni so far. In fact, she was speaking so fast that a huge cloud of her puffed words now hung over them. She sure was excited about being a bridesmaid!

Without warning Pheme changed the subject. "So, what was up with that Andromeda incident in Hero-ology this morning?"

Since Pheme had been in class and heard every-

138

thing, Medusa had expected the question sooner or later. But by now she'd learned to speak carefully around this girl. Because anything she said would be all over school in a flash. "Oh, that? That was no big deal," she replied, trying to downplay it.

"No big deal?" Pheme echoed, like she couldn't believe her ears. "Andromeda announces that she's the most beautiful princess in the sea, and you say it's no big deal? The sea world doesn't take such boasts kindly, you know."

Medusa looked at her in surprise. *That* was the incident she meant? Not Andromeda's crying fit because Medusa said she'd never be in the wedding? And not the blow-up between Dionysus and her? *Phew!*

When Pheme finally took a forkful of her nectaroni, Medusa sneakily batted away those last cloud-words that had risen from the girl's lips. She hoped no one else had

had time to read them. That's how rumors got started!

Whoosh! Suddenly the door to the cafeteria flew open and a strong gust of magic wind rushed in. *Summons for Medusa Gorgon!* it roared.

Every eye in the room turned toward Medusa, and several kids pointed in her direction. She held her breath. Was this wind going to deliver her Immortalizer necklace? Her excitement rose as the wind headed her way, swirling around students in its path and making them squeak in surprise as it tangled their hair and lifted the hems of tunics and chitons.

When it stopped at her table at last, the force of it blew away the remainder of Pheme's words. Then it imparted its message:

This command I bring your way—
It comes from the three Ladies Gray.

You must go to their office today.

You must depart without delay!

Await an escort in your room. . . .

Okay?

Medusa nodded. What else could she do? You couldn't disobey a summons from the Gray Ladies. They were the school counselors, and MOA rules said you had to drop everything and zip over to their office when called.

"Somebody's in trouble," Pheme sing-songed. "What did you do wrong?"

"Nothing," Medusa said defensively. "It's probably just a mistake." She'd never been called to the counselors' office before. Not even after she'd stolen Athena's Snakeypoo invention earlier in the year. But truthfully this summons could be about any number of

things—including Saturday's shoplifting. She gulped. Before Pheme could pump her for secrets, Medusa asked the wind, "Is that all? You didn't bring any packages for me?"

Packages? No!
Now away I blow!

With that the wind whooshed from the cafeteria again. "Were you expecting a package?" Pheme asked nosily.

Medusa jumped up. Pheme had a way of getting you to spill your guts if you weren't careful. She had to get out of there, fast. "No. Just thought I'd check. Take my tray to the return for me? I have to get going if I'm to catch my ride to the counselors!" Then she bolted off.

"Okay, but dress warmly!" Pheme called after her.

"Rumor has it that their office is in a distant land and it's freezing cold!"

Distant land? What a pain! thought Medusa as she took the stairs up to the dorms. That explained why an escort was being sent for her. As a mortal, long-distance travel was difficult. It was embarrassing that she couldn't whip around in a magic chariot or use the magic sandals like immortals could. Having to depend on others was the pits!

In her room she grabbed a long forest-green wool cape from her closet. Pulling both ends of the black ribbon tie at the neck of the cape, she yanked hard to fasten it shut. A long piece of ribbon snapped off.

Just then a knock came on the door. Stuffing the torn ribbon into her pocket, she called out, "Who's there?"

"Your ride to the Gray Ladies' office!" said a voice.

Athena? Sure enough, when Medusa opened the door a

143

crack, she saw Zeus's daughter standing in the hall. She was all bundled up in a wool cape too. Hers was blue-gray and matched the color of her eyes. Even though their rooms were only a few doors apart, Athena had never come to her room before, and vice versa.

Medusa quickly stepped into the hall so Athena wouldn't accidentally get a peek at her supercrush bulletin board. She locked the door behind her. "I guess your dad is making you give me a lift, huh? Like he made you help Heracles with his twelve labors that time?"

Athena's eyebrows rose. "That was supposed to be a secret."

"Pheme told me."

Athena let out an exasperated huff. "*Ye gods*, that girl finds out everything eventually! Well, we'd better head out."

Neither of them said another word till they reached

MOA's bronze front doors. Athena was probably annoyed because she had to take her, Medusa figured. Reaching into the big basket of winged sandals near the exit, they each grabbed a pair, and then slipped them on once they got outside.

The laces on Athena's sandals magically twined around her ankles and the silver wings at her heels began to flap. Gently she lifted a few inches from the ground. "What's wrong?" she asked, seeing Medusa's reluctance.

"You know I can't make these fly by myself, right?" Medusa gestured to her wing-sandaled feet, which were still firmly rooted to the ground.

"Yeah, I know." Athena reached out a hand. "C'mon."

Though she hated that she needed help in order to travel, Medusa took her hand. Immediately she rose to hover weightlessly above the ground as well.

Remembering the ribbon she'd stashed in her pocket, she pulled it out. Using her free hand and her teeth, she managed to use it to tie their wrists together.

"You don't have to do that. I won't let you fall," Athena promised.

Ignoring her, Medusa finished securely double-knotting the ribbon. "No offense," she said at last, "but I don't trust anybody." No way was she taking a chance that Athena might be planning to accidentally-on-purpose let go of her midflight. After all, the goddessgirl had been pretty mad at her when they'd talked outside the olive grove that morning.

"Whatever," said Athena, rolling her eyes. "Let's go!" And then they were off, skimming down the school steps. As they glided across the courtyard, the students they passed did double takes at seeing them together.

Medusa grinned. It wasn't every day that other kids saw her hanging out with one of the most popular goddessgirls in school!

Just beyond the courtyard Athena whipped out a papyrus scroll the magic wind had given her with directions to the counselors' office. The girls held it between them, studying it as they flew.

"These directions are so dumb!" Medusa grumped a while later. She read from the scroll: "'Fly north until you get goose bumps.'"

"In that case we must be getting close," Athena told her, shivering.

Realizing she was cold too, Medusa raised the hood of her cape to keep her snakes warm. By now the girls were flying high, their long capes billowing behind them. "We'd better find this place fast, or we'll turn into two nectar pops," she said.

147

Both girls looked down. Below them a gray-black sea churned. Floating icebergs dipped and rose in its choppy water. Medusa pointed to a building atop the largest iceberg. It looked like a giant upside-down bowl. An igloo! Carved into its roof were the words: "Office of the Gray Ladies."

Seeing it, Athena nodded. "Let's go down." The girls dipped, then slowed, their feet touching ground.

Medusa worked at the knotted ribbon that joined their wrists, freeing their hands. Then they started to walk. "Whoa!" she said as she slipped on the slick ice underfoot. She and Athena grabbed on to each other, trying to keep from falling.

Athena laughed. "It's like ice-skating!"

"Yeah, only I can't skate!" said Medusa. Fog swirled wildly around their legs as they slipped and slid their way to the opening of the igloo. They ducked inside its long tunnel entrance.

"It's warm in here," Athena said in surprise once they stood inside the main part of the igloo.

Medusa nodded. "I didn't expect an ice house to be so cozy." They were in some kind of little waiting room, and there was a door in the wall that she figured must lead to the actual counseling office beyond.

Both girls loosened their sandal straps and looped them around the silver wings to keep them still. Then they shrugged out of their capes and hung them on the coat hooks on the wall beside the only two chairs in the small room.

"Queen of Mean! You may enter!" three voices chorused in harmony. The girls jumped at the sound. Medusa shot Athena an embarrassed look before she scurried toward the door marked ENTER. Did the counselors know about her secret comics? she wondered nervously. And if so, what other secrets did they know about her?

"I'll be out here," Athena told her. Sinking into one of the chairs, she reached over to the side table, picked up a scrollazine called *Thrice the Advice*, and buried her nose in it.

Medusa opened the door and entered the counseling room. Inside there was no furniture, just three lumps of scraggly gray moss that looked kind of like haystacks. There was a small one, a middle-size one about Medusa's height, and a tall one.

"Hello?" she called, shutting the door behind her.

Suddenly the tall lump spoke. "Give me the eye!"

"What?" Medusa asked in surprise.

"The eye. Sisters, the eye! Who has it?"

At that a hand darted out from the smallest lump. It was holding a round white ball. With a squishy sound it popped the ball into the top part of what Medusa figured must be its face. Then the ball blinked at her. *Eww!* It was actually an *eye*ball! Its big gray iris looked her up and down.

"So you're the counselors—the Gray Ladies?" Medusa asked.

"What does she look like?" the tall lump asked, ignoring Medusa's question. "Oh, give me that thing so we can all get a look at her."

Squish! The small lump popped the eye out again. It was passed from gray lump to gray lump so each could stare at Medusa in turn.

These had to be the counselors, but they weren't made of moss or hay after all, Medusa realized. That scraggly, tangled gray stuff was their hair! It was so long, it dragged on the ground and completely hid them from view. And for some reason they shared only a single eyeball among them. Talk about weird!

Under their gaze Medusa was suddenly reminded of the Olympic Games when Artemis's brother Apollo had come up against the Python. That menacing serpent could read minds and had used the ability to defeat its competitors.

But counselors were supposed to help students, right? Not trick them. Then, why had they snooped into her mind and found out about her comics? Would these lump-ladies guess her most embarrassing secrets? Like her Poseidon crush? Her snakes' shoplifting? Her desire to be immortal and popular? She didn't trust them one bit!

The tall lump spoke up. "Don't be afraid to trust."

Medusa jerked her head back. Definitely reading

her mind! Which made these ladies not only weird and tricky but creepy, too! Her snakes curled in tight circles around her head, as if trying to form a cap that mind-reading waves couldn't penetrate.

Now the tall lump-lady plucked a white square from the center of her "face" and passed it to the middle lump, who stuck it onto her own face. It took Medusa a few seconds to realize that the square was actually a very large tooth. Not only did the lumps share a single eye among them, they also shared a single tooth! They passed the tooth around and were only able to speak when they stuck it into their mouths. Which made them not only weird, tricky, and creepy, but also dentally challenged.

"Don't be afraid to make friends," the middle lump suggested before passing the tooth to the small lump.

"Don't be afraid to be nice," it said, adding its two obols worth of advice.

Godzooks! Sure, Medusa didn't bother making friends or being nice, but it wasn't because she was *afraid* of those things. Was it? Whatever! She certainly didn't need these strange counselors telling her what to do.

"Can I go now?" she asked defiantly.

The Gray Ladies looked confused. What had they expected her to do? Bow down and thank them? Say something like, *Yeah, great idea! From now on I promise to be super-nice so that everyone will like me and want to be my friend?* No way!

Like most people, these lump-ladies just didn't get her. But at least they didn't seem to know all of her secrets, as far as she could tell. Maybe her snakes' mind-reading-proof cap was working.

"Go if you wish," said the small lump, who still had the tooth. "But think about what we said."

"Uh-huh," muttered Medusa. "I'll get right on that."

"Good," said the small lump, sounding pleased.

Like Medusa's own mom, these lump-ladies didn't seem to know sarcasm when they heard it. As she stomped out of the room, Sweetpea, her cuddliest snake, rubbed lightly against her cheek, trying to calm her.

"Let's go," Medusa told Athena, not looking at her.

"Can't. I'm next," Athena replied, putting aside her scrollazine and hopping up from the chair. At the same moment the three Ladies called out, "Daughter of Zeus! You may enter!"

"Huh?" Medusa stared in surprise as Athena walked past her through the small door and into the office. Since Athena hadn't contradicted her belief that Zeus had sent her only as an escort, Medusa had assumed she was right. But it looked like the Ladies must've commanded Athena to come here for counseling too! Why on Earth and Olympus would a brainy, pretty, popular goddessgirl like Athena need the advice of three weird, creepy, dentally challenged counselors?

There was one way to find out. Sneakily Medusa pressed her ear to the closed door. Unfortunately, Athena spoke too softly for her to hear what she said. But she *could* hear what the lump-ladies advised.

"Don't worry," said one of them. "Your dad won't love you any less just because he's getting married."

"Don't be afraid to talk your feelings over with him," said another one.

Were they crazy? Maybe they'd never met Zeus. He'd never struck Medusa as a let's-talk-about-our-feelings kind of guy. And if Athena was afraid that her dad would love her less once he married Hera, well, that seemed a reasonable fear to Medusa. After all, *her* parents only had enough love for her two sisters. She almost felt sorry for Athena. The advice the Gray Ladies were giving her was just as useless as the advice *she'd* been given.

When the doorknob turned unexpectedly, Medusa shot to a chair in one leap. Grabbing a scrollazine from the table, she tried to pretend she'd been sitting there all along instead of eavesdropping. "Ready to go?" she asked innocently when Athena appeared.

Athena nodded. Stepping outside, both girls freed the silver wings on their sandals and clasped hands. As the sandal wings began to flap, Medusa realized she'd forgotten to use the black ribbon to tie their wrists together. The tall lump-lady's words of advice floated into her mind: "Don't be afraid to trust." Well, maybe she'd try it, just this once.

Soon the girls were speeding back toward Mount Olympus Academy. Now and then Medusa sneaked peeks at Athena, trying to judge her mood, and hoping she hadn't been wrong to trust her.

"So do you think Hera will be a good stepmom?" she asked curiously after a while.

"I hope so," Athena said. If she'd guessed that Medusa had overheard what the Gray Ladies advised, she didn't say so.

"I think she'll be a lot better than some real moms I know, believe me," Medusa said. "And she seems to like you okay. I mean, her face softens when she looks at you." She wasn't trying to be nice. She was only telling the truth.

"Really?" asked Athena, glancing over at her.

"Yeah, trust me," said Medusa.

"Actually, I do," said Athena, sounding a little surprised by the fact. "One good thing about you is that you never act fake-nice. So if you say something nice, I always know you mean it." After a pause she added. "Thanks."

Athena was *thanking* her? Medusa couldn't believe it.

A warm feeling spread through her. It was a feeling that she usually got only when she was cuddling her snakes.

"Uh-huh," she mumbled. She so rarely got any praise that she wasn't quite sure how to react. The rest of the way back to MOA the girls chatted about those crazy haystack counselors, and the upcoming wedding, too. The time flew so quickly and Medusa was enjoying herself so much that she was kind of sorry when they landed in the courtyard.

Aphrodite, Persephone, and Artemis jumped up from the front steps of the school and waved to Athena. Had they been sitting there waiting for her the whole time she'd been gone? "See you later," Athena told Medusa, letting go of her hand. Then she zoomed off to be with her *real* friends.

"Bye," Medusa murmured under her breath. She felt a little hurt, even though she knew Athena wasn't being mean. It was just that for a while there she'd felt like she and Athena were friends too. Wouldn't it be great if they really were? *Don't be stupid,* she chided herself as she entered the Academy, climbed the marble stairs, and went to her room alone. Talk about an unrealistic dream!

Of course, little Andromeda's unrealistic dream *had* come true since Dionysus had made her a bridesmaid. But so far Medusa's dreams had only led to disappointment. Even so, there was one dream she refused to let go of—the Immortalizer necklace.

Unfortunately, over the next few days it failed to appear. As she waited for it to come, she continued to go to the gym each morning to faithfully swim her practice laps. And in Hero-ology she tried to make amends with her kindergarten buddy. However, Andromeda wasn't willing to forgive her so fast.

"Want to pet my snakes again?" Medusa offered on Tuesday. Andromeda looked like she wanted to, but then shrugged and shook her head no. On Wednesday Medusa suggested that they draw together, but her buddy was having none of it. By Thursday Medusa was almost ready to give up on the girl.

Don't be afraid to make friends, she remembered one of the Gray Ladies saying. Ha! You couldn't force someone to be your friend. Especially not a stubborn five-year-old!

9
Snake Face

*T*HUMP!

Medusa sat up in her bed and stared toward the open window, where the sudden sound had come from. There was something lying on her floor, just below the window-sill. A package! Had one of the magic winds brought the long-awaited necklace at last? By now it was Friday morning, almost a whole week since she'd ordered it.

She leaped out of bed and ran over. Plopping down on the floor in her sea-green pj's, she ripped the small box open. *Yes!* Inside was the Immortalizer. She gazed at it, dazzled by the delicate gold chain and dangly winged-horse charm. It was even more beautiful than the picture in the *Teen Scrollazine* ad!

Her hands trembled with excitement as she clasped it around her neck. Breathlessly she waited to turn into a goddessgirl. And waited. *Hmm.* She didn't feel any different. After a minute she dug around in the packaging for directions but couldn't find any. How did this thing work anyway?

Hey, maybe it had already made her immortal and she just didn't know it! Medusa jumped up and went over to her desk to test her magic powers. Pointing a finger at her red Hero-ology textscroll, she made a swirling motion. "Arise, scroll! And dance in the air!"

Nothing happened. Then she remembered that magic chants worked best when they rhymed. She tried again:

"Arise, scroll! And dance in the air.

For I am the girl with the snaky hair!"

It wasn't the best magical spell ever, but maybe it would work. *Or not,* she thought after a minute passed. After another minute went by and the scroll still hadn't budged, her shoulders drooped in disappointment.

Her skin hadn't begun to glitter softly as that of immortals did either. Reaching up, she stroked her snakes. "What do you think, guys? Is this necklace just a piece of junk?" Twister and Slinky gently looped themselves around her neck as if to say that even if the

Immortalizer was a dud, Medusa still had them, and they'd gladly volunteer to be her necklace.

"Thanks, guys," she said. "At least I can trust you to be there for me." She found the snake snack sack and tossed some dried peas into the air. All twelve reptiles eagerly snapped up their breakfast.

But so much for trusting in other stuff like those dumb counselors had advised her to do, she mused grumpily. She'd *trusted* that the necklace would really work, but it looked like this would turn out to be just one more doomed dream. She reached behind her neck to unclasp the necklace, then stopped.

Was she giving up too soon? What if the Immortalizer just took a while to have an effect? She had nothing to lose by continuing to wear it, right? It was pretty, after all.

As she changed out of her pj's, she willed the necklace to begin working by tomorrow morning. Because that's when Poseidon's contest was scheduled. With immortals in the race, she'd need the extra boost that magic could provide. Not only that, but Principal Zeus's wedding was only *two* days away! If the necklace started working right, she could create a thunderbolt holder for him that was even better than the one she'd seen in the Immortal Marketplace.

The necklace just *couldn't* fail her!

As Medusa slipped a chiton over her head, she imagined Principal Zeus gazing at her amazing thunderbolt holder gift with wonder in his eyes. She pictured him turning to her. *You're the greatest mortal to ever live,* he'd declare. *If anyone deserves immortality, it's you.* And then . . . She glanced at her Queen of Mean comic-scroll, wishing she had time to draw the whole scene.

But as she slipped on her sandals, the first lyrebell sounded. Oh, no! Class would be starting soon. No time for swim practice. She grabbed her textscroll and a breakfast power bar, then dashed downstairs to Hero-ology.

The minute she walked into class, she spotted Andromeda sitting across the room. Since all the guests would leave after the wedding, this was the last morning their kindergarten buddies would spend with them. Andromeda was so busy looking at the glittery pink princess storyscroll she held that she didn't even notice when Medusa came up to her. If she had, she probably would've run away. The girl really knew how to hold a grudge!

Medusa reached up and touched her winged-horse charm, moving it back and forth along the chain that held it. Deciding to test it again, she softly chanted a magic spell:

"Before this class comes to an end,

Make Andromeda be my friend!"

Instantly Andromeda glanced up from her story-scroll, her dark eyes going to the necklace. "Ooh! A pony. Can I see?" she asked, leaning closer.

She sounded so friendly. Maybe the Immortalizer really *was* starting to work! Medusa sat so the little girl could hold the charm and inspect it. There was a single name stamped into the metal on the back of the charm that she hadn't noticed until Andromeda turned it over. Medusa read it aloud. "Pegasus."

As in Pegasus, the winged horse? she wondered. He was one of the most popular fantastic creatures they'd ever studied in Beast-ology class. However, he'd been missing for so long that their teacher, Mr. Ladon, said he'd been reclassified as a myth or legend.

Andromeda quickly began spinning adventure stories about the horse, and Medusa joined in. Soon they were chatting away like friends, just as they had that first day. The change had happened so fast that surely it had to be magic. The necklace *must* be working, at least a little!

Pointing to the charm, Andromeda spoke to someone standing behind Medusa. "Look, Dionysus! A pony named Pegasus. Isn't he pretty?"

Medusa glanced up at the godboy.

"Yes, very pretty." He smiled down at Medusa, and her heart skipped a beat. For a second she'd thought he meant *she* was pretty. But of course he'd been referring to her Pegasus charm. He'd probably only smiled at her because he liked that she was getting along with her buddy again. Still, his smile had made her feel warm inside. Or was that just the spicy cinnamon in the power bar she'd gulped down on the way to class?

"How come you're not galloping around rescuing princesses this morning?" Medusa asked him.

He chuckled, his purple eyes sparkling. He had the longest eyelashes of any boy she'd ever met. "I'm still in my stable, I guess. Prince Perseus hasn't arrived yet. He's likely oversleeping in his castle."

"No, he's not. He's here, ready to fight evil!" shouted the little boy.

The three of them, along with most of the class, turned to see shaggy-haired Perseus grinning at them from the doorway. In a battle-ready stance he was brandishing a toy shield, and looking primed for another round of Princess Rescue.

Andromeda nudged Medusa, pointing. "Hey! Perseus's shield has your face on it!"

Startled, Medusa leaped to her feet and went to see the shield up close. That was her snake face all right.

170

And it was horrifying! The artist had painted her lips gold and had made her eyes red instead of pale green. And her snakes looked absolutely evil!

"Where on Earth did you get this?" she asked Perseus as she studied the embarrassing shield.

"My dad got it for me at that new store Be a Hero. It's demented, don't you think?" he asked, sounding delighted at the idea. "It's supposed to turn your enemies to stone. My dad says it's the most popular toy on Earth right now."

Her face was being used to scare people? How hurtful! But wait a minute—Perseus had said the shield was *popular*. Could this be the work of the necklace magic? She'd wanted popularity, after all. Only, this definitely wasn't the *cool* kind of popularity she'd had in mind!

Other students came over to examine Perseus's toy, including Athena, who took Medusa aside afterward.

"I can't believe you agreed to lend your image to this shield," she scolded quietly. "It's not only tacky, it's false advertising. You know that only you or your actual reflection can truly stone-ify a mortal."

So what? Medusa almost said. *I needed the money.* But even though she liked Athena more after their visit to the counselors, her own inner shield kept her from being honest. "What I do with my face is my business," she said instead. "Besides, Heracles lent his face to a sandwich!"

"He did not!" Athena said, hotly defending her crush. "He wouldn't do such a thing!"

Medusa smirked. "Ha! I saw it myself. In fact, I *ate* a sandwich with his picture on it. The Be a Hero store was selling them."

"Then, that's identity theft or . . . or copyright infringement!" Athena protested. "Something like that, anyway."

Most of the class had gathered around the shield

now, including Poseidon. Dionysus was there too, looking at the image on the shield, then back at Medusa, as
if comparing.

Medusa's cheeks heated. "What?" she snapped,
expecting an insult. Her snakes hissed, flicking their
tongues.

"Whoa, wait!" Dionysus held up both hands to ward
off their—and *her*—anger. "Before you and your snakes
bite my head off—"

"My snakes don't bite," Medusa informed him in a
superior tone. "Unless ordered to."

Though she'd been trying to unnerve him, Dionysus
just smiled. "Got it. But all I was thinking a minute ago
was that you're way prettier than that image of you on
the shield. I mean, the artist was an idiot! Your eyes are
green, not red. Duh."

Medusa folded her arms and sent him a disbelieving

173

gaze. Was that a compliment? She wasn't sure. Maybe it was really just veiled sarcasm. But if it *was* a genuine compliment, she hoped Poseidon had overheard. It wouldn't hurt for him to get a teeny bit jealous.

Looking over, she saw that Poseidon's attention was on his buddy, though. Andromeda and Perseus had started playing Princess Rescue again. Poseidon smiled broadly when Andromeda yelled out in mock terror, "Help! Help! Save me!"

"Hold on," Perseus called to her. "I'm coming!"

Maybe Andromeda has the right idea, Medusa thought. Godboys liked to feel strong. Just look how they'd all oohed and aahed over the twelve labors Heracles had accomplished a while back. Did boys really prefer girls who were helpless? Was that the main reason Poseidon had never fallen in like with her—because she was too strong and self-sufficient?

Her eyes shifted back to Dionysus, who was staring at her with the oddest look on his face. "Do you think I come on too strong?" she asked.

"What?" He laughed in surprise. Seeing she was serious, he looked more thoughtful, then nodded. "Sometimes."

Before she could ask what that meant, Poseidon called him over. However, as Dionysus turned to leave, she thought she heard him add, "But I like it."

She shook her head to clear it. There must be something wrong with her ears! Dionysus starred in just about every school drama. With his violet eyes, cute dimples, and sweet smile, he was *handsome.* And there was no shortage of girls at MOA who practically drooled over him every time he walked by. As she watched him join in the game with Poseidon and their buddies, a weird feeling came over her. A liking feeling.

No! What was she thinking? She preferred godboys with turquoise skin.

Didn't she?

At lunch Medusa wolfed down a heaping bowl of ambrosia stew and a carton of nectar, then stared at her hands expectantly. Although the "food of the gods" didn't have the desired effect of making her skin immediately shimmer, she refused to give up hope that the Immortalizer was starting to work.

After all, her other wishes had begun coming true. Andromeda was her friend again, and the shield had made her popular (or at least infamous!).

And that very afternoon, when she was on her way to fourth-period Revenge-ology class—her best subject— another of her dreams came true. Principal Zeus *noticed* her. Only not in the way she'd hoped.

"You, with the snakes!" he shouted at her in the hall. "Follow me." Turning on one big sandal, he headed toward the front office.

"Ye gods," she muttered as she trudged after him. If he'd heard about the shoplifting, she was doomed. Automatic expulsion.

All nine of Ms. Hydra's heads stared at the two of them as they went through to Zeus's office, but Medusa hardly noticed. Was she about to be banned from MOA forever? Sent back to Earth? *Nooo!* She racked her brain for some excuse that might save her.

While tromping across his messy office, Zeus stepped on a stack of folders, squashed an Olympusopoly game box underfoot, and then stubbed his toe on a dented file cabinet that was lying on its side in the middle of the floor.

"Ow! Ow!" Hopping on one foot, he managed to

make it over to his desk. He plopped down on the enormous golden throne behind it. Any other time Medusa would've found Zeus's clumsiness funny, but right now she felt like a prisoner going to her execution.

The second she sat in the small chair across the desk from him, Zeus slammed his meaty fist down on his desktop. Sparks flew from between his fingers but quickly fizzled out. "What's this I hear about you licensing your image for mean-spirited products? That's not who we are at MOA. We have standards, a reputation to uphold here."

Huh? She hadn't expected *this*. How had Principal Zeus found out about the shield this fast, anyway? Of course, anyone in Hero-ology class might've brought it to his attention. Or maybe he'd come across the shield himself—it was *popular*, after all.

To her horror Medusa felt tears fill her eyes. All in all it had been a pretty horrible week, and she'd had enough of people being mad at her for stuff that wasn't really her fault. Who could've guessed that Mr. Dolos would use her image to scare people?

Watching her, Zeus's eyes widened in a *yikes* sort of way. He backed his throne away from his desk so fast, it almost toppled over. "Wait. You aren't going to cry, are you?"

Talk about being uncomfortable with feelings! Those Gray Ladies were crazy for advising Athena to talk to her dad about how she felt.

Medusa sat up straight, determined to keep a stiff upper lip. But the thought of being kicked out of MOA was too overwhelming, and suddenly her defenses crumbled. To her horror the tears she'd been struggling to hold back rolled down her cheeks. "I licensed my image because I needed money," she blurted. "To buy a wedding gift for you and Hera, and also for—"

"Now, now, stop your blubbering," he begged. If someone else had been doing the crying instead of her, it would've cracked her up to watch him acting this way. Zeus—who was seven feet tall and the biggest, baddest ruler in Olympus—couldn't handle one sobbing student?

But she couldn't stop crying. It was like a dam had burst behind her eyeballs, unleashing a flood of tears. "I didn't know my image would be used on a shield and customers would be told it would turn their enemies to stone," she went on between sobs. "I only thought Mr. Dolos would put my face on a wheel of Gorgonzola cheese or something. Honest. I didn't know I was doing anything wrong."

"Mr. Dolos?" Zeus echoed in surprise. His eyes narrowed.

Medusa swiped at her tears with the back of her hand. "You've heard of him?"

With a big sigh Zeus ran his fingers through his wild red hair, making it stand up straight like it had been electrified. "Yeah, that guy is a sleaze. He's so wily he could even trick an immortal into buying a fake thunderbolt!" He sent her an embarrassed glance. "Um . . . at least that's what I've heard."

Medusa held her breath, allowing herself to hope that he wasn't going to kick her out of MOA after all. So far he hadn't mentioned shoplifting. "Um, are you still mad at me?" she asked finally.

"Mad? I guess not. The shield was just the final straw." He frowned, then spoke as if to himself. "Problem's really all this wedding business. Party planning is not my thing."

"Maybe you need a vacation. A little time to cool off," Medusa dared to suggest. She could hardly believe she was giving advice to the King of the Gods! But then, the

Gray Ladies handed out advice all the time, and they were certainly not whizzes at it, if you asked her.

The principal shook his head. "No can do. Hera needs me. I promised to go to her store this afternoon to pick up balloons and ribbons and stuff for the wedding on Sunday." He shivered, as if the idea of getting involved with decorations was a fate worse than death.

"Why don't you ask Athena to go with you?" Medusa suggested. "I bet she'd love to help with the decorating."

"Theeny?" Zeus rubbed his beard, looking thoughtful. "You know, it's been far too long since I've spent much time with my brainy girl. Maybe I'll take her with me to Hera's store. What a great idea! Glad I thought of it." Jumping up, Zeus yelled, "Cancel my appointments, Ms. Hydra! I'm off to see my favorite daughter of all time!"

Ms. Hydra's happiest head—the sunny yellow one— poked around the door frame. "Certainly, sir," she replied cheerfully. Then the head withdrew to snap back into place among her other eight heads.

Wow! Athena is going to be thrilled, thought Medusa as Principal Zeus headed out of the office. And since he thought it was all his idea, Athena would never know that she had actually suggested it. But, of course, she hadn't meant to do anything nice for Athena. Not really. The idea had just popped into her head. Like magic. Obviously it was more evidence that the Immortalizer was working!

Medusa rose from her chair to go. But then, seeing that Ms. Hydra wasn't paying any attention to her, she changed her mind. Tiptoeing over to Zeus's throne, she sat in it just for fun. Kicking back, she crossed her feet on the desktop. Then she studied the office in detail, trying to memorize it so she could draw it in her next Queen of Mean comic-scroll episode. Noticing a stack of wedding scrollazines on Zeus's desk that Hera must've left, she picked up an issue of *Goddess Bride Guide* and stared dreamily at the bride and bridesmaids on its cover.

"I hope you guys don't mind wearing orange roses," she murmured to her snakes. "Because I think this necklace I bought is starting to work. Which means I'm going to win that swimming contest tomorrow. Which means I'm going to be a bridesmaid. And that means we're going to march down the aisle with Poseidon!"

She sighed happily.

10

The Contest

THE NEXT MORNING MEDUSA PUT ON HER

swimsuit and hurried to the underground pool in the

grotto below the MOA gymnasium. Poseidon's contest

was about to begin!

The rows of stone seats on one side of the pool were

already full of students who'd come to watch. Most of the

godboys were there, but she didn't see Dionysus. Athena,

Aphrodite, Artemis, and Persephone were in the stands, though, and Athena smiled and waved in her direction. Medusa ignored her, figuring she was waving at someone else—a *real* friend.

As she did stretches to warm up for her swim, Medusa sized up the competition. About half the girls were mortals and half were immortals. Some were the daughters of wedding guests, and the rest were MOA students. Including Pandora. Huh? Was that girl crazy? She couldn't even swim without floaties. At least she'd had the sense to wear some on her arms. They would slow her down, though. She was dreaming if she thought she had any chance of winning.

Only one girl was going to win the honor of being Poseidon's bridesmaid in Zeus's wedding. And her name started with *M, As in Marvelous, Magnificent, Me!* thought Medusa, her spirits rising.

She touched the Pegasus charm at her throat, making sure her Immortalizer necklace was still in place. Doing arm circles to loosen her muscles, she let her gaze casually drift over to her supercrush.

Trident in hand, Poseidon was busy using his magic to redesign the racecourse. For today's competition he'd shaped the pool into an enormous octagon filled with sparkling turquoise water. To make the contest harder, he'd added obstacles, including dolphin statues that actually leaped and frolicked, sea horse fountains spouting water, and a big blue rock island in the center of the pool.

The swimmers were supposed to circle the rock island to a finish line, which was made of twisted strands of pearls and semiprecious aquamarine jewels. By her estimation it wouldn't take more than five minutes for her to reach it. Then the race would be over!

Hearing childish giggles, Medusa looked upward to the bridge Poseidon had created to span the pool. It arched over the rock island, and its sides were tiled with bits of shells that formed a mosaic of scenes from Poseidon's realm—the sea. There were mosaic coral reefs, brightly colored fish, and sea beasts that looked so real they almost seemed to move.

Some of the kindergarten buddies were sitting or standing atop the bridge to watch the race, including Cetus, Andromeda, and Perseus, as well as some older kids. Medusa waved to Andromeda, and she waved back.

"Swimmers!" Poseidon called out, drawing her attention. "On your marks."

Medusa quickly traded her stoneglasses for stonegoggles, which were swim goggles that would keep her from turning any mortals to stone while in the water. Then she went to stand poolside, shoulder to shoulder with the other racers. Her snakes wove themselves tight, forming a sort of swimming cap on her head.

As she gazed at Poseidon's handsome profile, a sigh escaped her. Couldn't he see they were perfect for one another? She was an amazing swimmer; he was god of the sea. Most seas had serpents in them, which were pretty much like giant snakes. And she had snake hair. Duh. They had so much in common, it wasn't even funny!

"Get set!" Poseidon called out. All the swimmers crouched forward.

If she believed in the necklace's magic—had a little more *trust* that it would work—would that help? It couldn't hurt. Medusa grabbed the charm on her necklace in one fist. Squinching her eyes shut, she said a magic wish spell under her breath. "Let me win. Let me win." It wasn't a rhyme, but she didn't have time to think of one!

"Go!" shouted Poseidon, raising his trident high.

SPLASH! The competitors dove in.

Medusa used strong, steady strokes and was soon in the lead. *This will be over in no time!* she thought gleefully. But as she circled the rock island, she noticed that the finish line kept moving farther away. Poseidon was adjusting it backward from time to time to make the race last longer. At least he could have warned them he was going to do that! Around and around they all swam. When her head popped out of the water on a breathing stroke, she saw Pandora sitting poolside. She'd bailed out of the race already. So had some others. Yay!

Eventually the finish line stopped moving away. It was only thirty yards ahead now. Determined, Medusa put on a burst of speed, widening her lead. Victory was almost hers.

Distantly she heard Andromeda shout, "Save me!"

Figuring it was just another game of Princess Rescue, Medusa kept swimming. But on her next stroke she noticed something moving on the rock island below the bridge in the center of the pool. Andromeda? How had she gotten down there?

"Help! Help!" the little girl screamed. She must've fallen. Or maybe she'd been pushed! Though Medusa continued to swim, each time she lifted her head to breathe, she peeked over her shoulder.

Splash! Splash! Splash! Cetus and some of the other sea serpents and sea nymphs dove into the pool. They all sprouted fishtails the minute they hit the water and were now swimming around the rock island like sharks.

"Take back what you said the other day!" Cetus was shouting at Andromeda.

"Yeah. No way you're prettier than us," called the nymphs. Flipping their tails, they splashed Andromeda with a high wave, drenching her. "Everyone knows that sea creatures are the most beautiful of all!"

Medusa faltered in her stroke, and the other swimmers gained on her. Why wasn't anyone stopping this? she wondered. But all the swimmers left in the race had already passed the rock and were now on their final lap. And the crowd was busy cheering on their favorite swimmers. No one else seemed to have noticed what was going on. Or maybe they thought the kids were just playing.

She looked ahead to the finish line, agonizing about what to do. Keep swimming, or go back to perform a *real* princess rescue? Then, with a sigh that came out as more of a gurgle since she was in the water, she turned and swam toward the rock island. The other swimmers raced past, going the opposite direction toward the finish line.

"You're not a pretty princess," one of the teenage sea serpents was taunting Andromeda. "You're a scaredy-cat!"

"No! She's pretty, all right. *Pretty* afraid of the water," another yelled. They all laughed, whipping their tails to splash her.

"Stop it, you meanies! I can't swim!" Hugging the big rock, Andromeda stubbornly refused to take back her words, or maybe she was just too scared to think straight.

Just then little Perseus made a brave attempt to rescue her from the bullies. Climbing from the bridge onto the rock, he made his way down to stand in front of Andromeda protectively. Showing the serpents his Medusa shield, he said, "Back off or turn to stone, foes!"

"Ha-ha! Those shields don't work!" called one of the older nymphs. "They're fake. Just like Andromeda is a fake princess!"

"I'm a *real* princess!" Andromeda insisted, crying now.

Medusa zoomed through the water faster and faster. She was not going to let the little girl be taunted one minute longer! She dove deep and then came up right in the middle of the sea bullies. Staring them down, she announced, "The shields may not work, but my real gaze works just fine. In three seconds I'm going to whip off these goggles. And that means you'd better scram if you don't want to be stone-ified. One . . . two . . ."

Instantly the sea creatures turned tail and fled.

Medusa reached for Andromeda and Perseus. "Come on, you two. I'll swim you over to the side." It turned out that Perseus could swim on his own, but it took her a few minutes to coax Andromeda into the water. Looping an arm around her, Medusa did a one-armed sidestroke, taking her to the edge of the pool.

By now the race was over. The audience had finally noticed what had happened on the rock, and some had gathered to help them climb out.

A staff artist for the *Greekly Weekly News* appeared

with a scroll in hand. Staring at her and Andromeda, he began busily sketching with his quill pen. Why was he drawing a picture of them? Medusa wondered. Wasn't he supposed to be sketching a likeness of the race's winner?

Then she realized that his job was probably to cover anything related to tomorrow's wedding, which included bridesmaids. And of course Andromeda would be one of those. But *she* wouldn't. Because in helping her kindergarten buddy, Medusa had lost the race.

Someone handed her stoneglasses to her, and she swapped them for the stonegoggles she was wearing. She didn't know who'd won the race, and she didn't care. Neither did the crowd, it seemed. Most everyone had gathered around her, Andromeda, and Perseus. Spotting Poseidon standing nearby, Medusa pushed through the crowd toward him. He was holding a crown of pretty white sea asters meant for the winner of his contest.

"Why weren't you watching out for those little kids?" she demanded in a voice that echoed around the grotto. The crowd hushed to listen in, but she didn't even notice. "They could have drowned, you know! How could you be so careless?"

"You're right, you're right. Sorry about that," Poseidon said. Glancing around at everyone watching, he smiled and waved. He didn't seem to be taking this at all seriously! "Hey," he added, winking at the onlookers, "no harm done, right? And wasn't Medusa amazing out there? A real hero! Let's give her a hand. Woo-hoo!"

Sliding the sea aster crown over his arm like an oversize bracelet so both hands were free, he began clapping for her. His enthusiasm was so great that everyone else joined in. The applause was nice, but she wasn't anywhere near ready to forgive him.

There was a sea nymph standing nearby who didn't

196

look too thrilled either. The race winner, Medusa guessed. The girl was dripping wet with a towel over her shoulders, and she was gazing at Poseidon as if willing him to notice her. Medusa knew exactly how it felt to yearn for his attention. She'd been doing it for years.

"Aren't you going to announce the name of your bridesmaid?" Medusa asked, gesturing toward the nymph.

"Oh, sure, in a sec," Poseidon said, shrugging. He leaned closer. "But first I wanted to say that, between you and me, I really wish you'd won. You were in the lead most of the race. You deserved it," he said in an admiring voice too soft to reach the crowd. But it was loud enough for the nymph to overhear. An embarrassed expression flickered across her face.

Medusa cringed. Poseidon was being incredibly rude! He didn't seem to care about the nymph's feelings one bit.

"You know, I don't have to stick around with my bridesmaid after the ceremony tomorrow," he went on. "Want to save me a dance? And maybe hang out?"

Gazing into Poseidon's gorgeous turquoise eyes, Medusa wondered why she wasn't jumping for joy. This was what she wanted, right? His attention focused on her? He was acting like he liked her. Why didn't it feel as good as she'd expected? Maybe it was because of that sea nymph hovering behind him, looking uncertain and hurt. Hadn't she felt that same way herself too many times to count?

Someone handed her a fresh towel, and she began drying off her snakes. Poseidon's gaze rose to the top of her head, and his nose scrunched up like he'd just smelled something barfy. "Just one thing," he murmured, flashing his patented cute-guy smile. "Could you maybe wear a hat tomorrow, or a veil? To, you know, hide your hair?"

Anger rose in Medusa, swift and hot. Maybe her sisters could get away with saying stuff like that to her because they were, well, her sisters. But where did he get off? She stared at him, feeling like she was seeing the real him for the first time. Her snakes froze, waiting to see what she'd do—whether she'd stick up for them or not. Well, nobody insulted her snakes and got away with it!

She stepped right up to Poseidon and jabbed a fingertip into his chest. "You know what you are?" she said. "An ophidiophobiac!"

"Huh? I am not," he said, sounding flustered. It was obvious he had no idea what an ophidiophobiac was.

"It means that even though you rule the mighty serpents of the sea, you're scared of my little snakes!" said Medusa.

"Am not!" he protested.

"Are too. You even admitted it to me once," said a

girl's voice. Medusa glanced over and saw that it was Athena who'd spoken. She and her friends were standing nearby, comforting Andromeda. It looked like everyone had been listening to their argument.

"Well, who *isn't* icked out by your snakes?" Poseidon defended himself. "Ask any godboy if he'd like to hang out with a girl with wiggling, hissing hair! I don't *think* so!"

For the first time Medusa realized how shallow Poseidon was. Had he always been this way? she wondered. Why hadn't she ever noticed before? Maybe she'd been blinded by that amazing smile he'd given her when she'd first come to MOA. But she supposed someone could be friendly and still be shallow.

"All I'm asking is that you keep your hair under wraps for the wedding. No big deal, right? So, c'mon, what do you think?" Poseidon asked. Though he moved closer to her, he seemed to be staring at someone behind her.

She looked over her shoulder and saw the artist from the *Greekly Weekly News* who'd been drawing her picture earlier. He was still drawing. And Poseidon was trying to get into the picture too!

"I'll tell you what I think," she told Poseidon. She paused to slip on her sandals, and then glared at him, giving her towel a sharp tug as she tied it around her waist. "I think you are self-centered beyond belief. And you know what else I think? I think you should take that trident of yours and stick it up your nose, fishboy!"

Whirling around, she stalked out of the gym, past the sports fields, through the courtyard, and into the Academy, leaving a trail of water droplets in her path. Poseidon had crushed her supercrush with his lack of consideration for her snakes, Andromeda, and even the sea nymph who'd won his contest. Now *she* was going to do a different kind of crushing.

Upstairs in her dorm room she slammed the door and went straight for her supercrush bulletin board. She yanked all the stuff off it and stomped on the bits and pieces, pulverizing everything she'd collected for years. Then she tossed the mashed-up remains into her trash can and just stood there feeling horrible.

When she reached up to pet her snakes, they gently curled and uncurled around her wrists. "You're right, guys," she told them. "He is so not worth it." Still, her crush had been in her thoughts for so long that she felt kind of lonely all of a sudden. What would she spend her free time doing now? She couldn't study *all* the time.

Hearing a commotion outside her window, Medusa glanced down at the courtyard four stories below. Hermes had just landed his chariot. As she watched, Dionysus stepped out of the back of it carrying a big mailbag over one shoulder. Something was squirming inside it.

Suddenly his face turned up, looking toward her window. She dropped to a crouch below the window-sill. *Ye gods!* Had he seen her? She hoped not. She was a mess—all drippy from her swim. Then she noticed that her curious snakes were standing tall, still peeking out the window glass above her. She tugged them down too.

What was in that mailbag Dionysus was carrying? she wondered. A magical wedding gift for Zeus and Hera? Hey! In all the excitement she'd practically forgotten about her necklace! Now was a good time for the ultimate test of its magic. She would use it to make her own gift—or try to. Her fingers touched the chain, then twisted it round and round, searching for the winged horse charm that dangled from it. But it was gone!

Oh, no! Could it have come off in the pool? Still in her swimsuit and towel, she retraced her steps to the gym. Head down, she searched the ground along the way, just in case. When she reached the grotto, it was empty and the pool itself had already been redesigned into a heart shape for tomorrow's wedding.

Poseidon had filled it with floating flowers, and their delicate scent filled the air. Kneeling at the edge of the pool, Medusa pushed some of the blossoms aside and peered into the watery depths to look for the charm.

Was that a glint of gold? Yes! There it was, lying on the bottom! She dove in and recovered it. Sitting poolside, she held the charm in one fist and made up a rhyme she hoped would work. It was now or never.

> *"Necklace magic,*
>
> *Come forth and bring*
>
> *A magical gift, fit for a king.*
>
> *A holder of thunderbolts, strong and true.*
>
> *Wing it my way, without further ado!"*

Ado? Ha! She'd stolen the MOA herald's favorite word! But as the minutes passed and nothing happened, her dream of creating a fabulous wedding gift was slowly crushed. Just as thoroughly as the stuff from her bulletin board had been. And if the necklace magic didn't work for making a gift, it surely wasn't going to make her immortal.

She yanked off the necklace chain and hurled both it and the charm into the pool. Watching them sink to the bottom, she felt her heart and hopes sink with them. Along with her dreams, unrealistic or not.

11

Sisters, Enemies, and Friends

YOU OWE US FIFTEEN ROOM CLEANINGS," Stheno announced two hours later as the triplets were finishing up their lunch in the cafeteria at their usual table.

This unjust claim jerked Medusa out of her funk. "No way! I only promised to do it one time," she protested. She licked the lime-green nectar pop she'd chosen for dessert.

"That was before we did you a huge favor," Euryale informed her.

"What favor?"

"We fixed things at Gods Gift," said Stheno. "After you shoplifted."

Medusa's eyes widened. "How? I mean, when? I mean, I didn't shoplift—"

"Yeah, yeah, tell it to the judge," Euryale said, cutting her off. "We got there just after you left the store, and we used our magic to make all those freaky gift box puppets forget they'd ever met you."

"The guards too," added Stheno. "And so now, we figure you owe us fifteen room cleanings. That's for two guards plus twelve puppets, plus the trip to the marketplace that day."

After a minute Medusa nodded. Truthfully, she was mega-relieved she wouldn't have to worry about that whole shoplifting *incident* anymore. Her place at MOA was secure. Still, it would have been nice if her sisters had told her sooner. How like them to make her sweat a while!

Suddenly she spied Dionysus across the cafeteria. To her surprise he waved her over.

"Dusa and Dionysus sittin' in a tree," Stheno teased softly.

"K-I-S-S-I-N-G," Euryale finished.

"Oh, shut up," Medusa muttered, rolling her eyes. Still licking her nectar pop, she went to see what he wanted.

"I have a present for you," he told her, leading her outside. "Brought it up in Hermes' chariot this morning."

Curious, Medusa followed him out of the cafeteria and then stopped midlick. A few feet away was the big squirmy mail sack she'd seen from her dorm window earlier. Dionysus undid its drawstring, and out popped

Mr. Dolos! She stared at the little round man with his slicked-back hair and stiffly curled mustache. "What are you doing here?"

"I brought him," Dionysus replied.

"In a mail sack?" Medusa asked, feeling confused.

"Sacking him up was the only way to make him stop trying to convince Hermes to license his image for a new line of chariot-shaped footwear. For a while there I thought Hermes would toss him out midflight."

Mr. Dolos shrugged. "What can I say? I'm a business-man."

"No," Medusa said. "What you are is a liar." She gave her nectar pop a flick, pointing it at him. Little green drops accidentally splattered on the front of his yellow-and-black-checkered tunic.

"Who, me?" Mr. Dolos glanced down at the green drops in dismay, then looked back up at Medusa. "I've done nothing wrong." But despite his words she could see in his eyes that he knew he wasn't really telling the truth. He didn't care who he hurt as long as he made money!

"Don't blame me if you're disappointed in our deal," he said defensively. "Didn't you read the fine print in your contract?"

"No," she admitted, "but you didn't really give me a chance to."

Mr. Dolos twirled the ends of his mustache. "Or maybe you were in too much of a hurry to get me to hand over the thirty drachmas."

Dionysus raised an eyebrow at that. Medusa hoped he didn't think she was greedy. "But the shields don't even work," she protested. "There's no magic in them at all."

"Doesn't matter," Mr. Dolos insisted. "What matters is

that my customers *think* they're magic. Makes them feel like heroes. Gives them confidence. And isn't that what we need to defeat our enemies?"

Medusa didn't think his logic was sound, but before she could object, he went on. "Oh, I almost forgot. Here you go." Reaching into the mail sack at his feet, he pulled out a bag of drachmas. She was so surprised, she took it. "It's your share of the earnings. I told you you'd be a best-seller."

Medusa felt the weight of the coins. There must be a hundred drachmas in the bag! With this she could buy a great wedding gift. But money couldn't buy the immortality she craved. And if she took the bag, wouldn't it be like she was agreeing that it was okay for Mr. Dolos to do whatever he wanted with her image? That it was okay to lie to his customers about the shield being magic?

"No deal." She shoved the money back into his hands.

Yet Mr. Dolos hardly noticed. His eyes had widened at something beyond her. "Whatever. Gotta run now!" he shouted as Zeus thundered after him.

"Come back here, you thief!" yelled the principal. "That thunderbolt you sold me was about as real as a purple unicorn!" Zeus chased after him, zinging the little man with tiny bursts of electricity that made Mr. Dolos yelp.

Medusa grinned at Dionysus as they watched them go. "Who knows? Maybe this will be just the *spark* Mr. Dolos needs to change his business practices!"

Dionysus laughed, showing his dimples. "Oh, greenie girl, you crack me up like nobody else. 'Spark'—ha-ha-ha! I love it!"

And suddenly Medusa felt a spark of something herself. A spark of joy mixed with liking that equaled crushing. Not supercrushing—not yet. But definitely crushing. "Thanks. I think," she said casually, trying to push the feeling away. She wasn't ready to get her heart broken *again*.

Bam, bam, bam!

Medusa sat up in bed. It was the next morning, and someone was knocking on her door. Out of habit she called out, "Go away!"

"Open up!" Athena called back.

"Yeah, c'mon!" said Aphrodite.

Medusa's brows rose. What could they possibly want? Her eyes went to the trash can. Since the Poseidon stuff she'd collected was gone from the wall, there was no harm in letting them in, she supposed. But on her way to the door, she shoved the trash can into her closet, just to be on the safe side. She'd die if they saw all that super-crush junk!

"Look!" said Athena, practically dancing with excitement as she burst in. "You're in the *Greekly Weekly News!*" She held the news-scroll open so they could all see it.

Medusa stared at the headlines. "'Zeus to Wed Hera in Ceremony Today at Noon'?" she read in confusion.

"No, not that headline," said Aphrodite. She pointed to another story a little farther down. "Here."

Medusa sucked in her breath. "Oh!" Right below the main story about the upcoming wedding was a big, dramatic sketch showing her rescue of Andromeda! The news of Poseidon's swimming competition was way down in one corner, and there was only a small picture of him and the nymph who'd won.

"Not everyone gets on the front page of *GW!*" exclaimed Aphrodite.

"Epic," said Medusa, glowing with pleasure.

Athena glanced around the room. "Want to hang it on your bulletin board? Looks like you've got space for it."

Medusa nodded. Kneeling on her spare bed, she tacked the news-scroll up. It helped fill some of the empty space where all her Poseidon stuff used to be. They all three stared at it for a few seconds, admiring it.

Finally Aphrodite nudged Athena. "C'mon. We've got a wedding to get ready for!" She started out the door, but Athena held back a minute. "My dad and I picked up some wedding decorations from Hera's shop on Friday," she said to Medusa. "And he told me you'd suggested that he ask for my help."

"He did?" Medusa grimaced, bracing herself for Athena's annoyance at her interference.

Athena grinned sideways at her. "Ha! I guessed right!"

Medusa stared at her, unsure. "So you're not mad I butted in?"

"No, it's okay," Athena went on. "He didn't really tell me it was your idea—he thought it was his. But I had a feeling—"

"So how did it go?" interrupted Medusa.

Athena smiled broadly now, looking lighter than she had all week. "We had a good talk, and I even hung out with Hera while we were getting the decorations. So, thanks. You kind of helped break the ice between us all."

"Really?"

"Really."

Aphrodite poked her head back into the room. "Sorry," she said to Athena. "I thought you were right behind me." Medusa wondered how much of their conversation she'd overheard.

The two goddessgirls exchanged glances, and some

silent message flew between them. When Aphrodite nodded, Athena turned back to Medusa. "Listen, we promised to help Persephone and her mom with the flowers before the wedding. Want to help too?"

It was on the tip of Medusa's tongue to say no. She had studying to do, as always. Besides, what if Athena was only asking because she thought she *owed* Medusa for helping her out with her dad? But then she thought about the Gray Ladies and their advice about trusting and making friends and being nice. Maybe their suggestions weren't as lame as she'd first thought. And maybe she could take a day off from studying for once.

"Okay, sure. I think I'd be good with flowers," she said at last. Then she held out her hands. "After all, I have *two* green thumbs!"

When the goddessgirls laughed, she joined in. Dionysus was right, thought Medusa. She was hilarious!

"Change out of your pj's then, and meet us in my room," Aphrodite told her. "We need to grab our bridesmaid gowns to put on later in the gymnasium changing rooms, just before the wedding."

Medusa dressed quickly, donning her very best emerald-green chiton and matching sandals. Minutes later she, Athena, and Aphrodite were heading across the courtyard. Stheno and Euryale were sitting outside on one of the marble benches, reading the *Greekly Weekly News*. As Medusa walked by, they glanced up, looking stunned that she—a mortal—had made the front page. And now she was hanging out with two of the most popular goddessgirls at MOA!

Medusa just smiled serenely and waggled her fingers in a little wave. And, if she wasn't mistaken, her sisters' faces turned ever so slightly greener. Was this how it felt to be popular? If so, she loved it!

12
The Wedding Gift

WHEN MEDUSA, ATHENA, AND APHRODITE
entered the gymnasium, they all gasped at the trans-
formation. "It's an enchanted wedding paradise," Aphrodite cooed. Since she was the goddessgirl of love, her
praise of weddings was often exaggerated. But in this
case she was right. Everything was so beautiful!

The gym building, which was round, had been

decorated to look like a giant wedding cake. Fluffy white swirls of plaster that resembled frosting covered the walls. Nestled in it here and there were sculpted pink hearts and orange rosettes. The circular opening in the ceiling revealed a bright blue sky dotted with happy, puffy clouds.

In the middle of the gym floor on a raised stage stood a ten-foot-tall wedding arch draped with swags of white netting. The two goddessgirls sighed at the sight of it. Even Medusa, who usually scoffed at anything frou-frou, couldn't help being impressed. At the top of the arch and on both of its sides, the netting was gathered and tied with curly ribbons and fragrant orange blossoms. This was where Zeus and Hera would stand when they exchanged wedding vows.

Rows of white chairs had been lined up on either side of a single aisle that led from the gym door to the stage.

Beyond the chairs, the bleachers had been replaced by dozens of linen-draped tables. Elaborate floral arrangements sat at the center of some of the tables, each with a glittery, decorative three-foot-long thunderbolt sticking up from the middle of the flowers at an artful angle. Seeing Persephone and her mom busily constructing more of the centerpieces for the remaining empty tables, the three girls rushed over to assist.

While they were working, the first guests began to arrive. Artemis was among them, and most of the kindergarten buddies too. Medusa slipped her stoneglasses out of her pocket and put them on. She cringed when she saw that Perseus was still carrying his toy shield with the embarrassing picture of her face. And she tried not to notice the long tables off to one side that were soon overflowing with fabulous wedding gifts—not one of them from her.

Just as the girls finished placing the last table centerpiece, trumpetlike horns called salpinxes blared. The MOA herald and several musicians had come to stand on the steps leading up to the stage. At this signal everyone scurried for the chairs on either side of the aisle.

"See you later," Persephone told her mom. She, Athena, and Aphrodite dashed off to change into their bridesmaid dresses. Medusa went to grab a good seat.

A few minutes later the horns trumpeted again. Zeus appeared and crossed the stage, coming to stand under the arch. Wearing formal attire in MOA colors—a gold tunic with a flowing gold and blue cape—he stood gazing down the long empty aisle toward the door, waiting.

Guest musicians seated just beyond the stage began to play softly. Dionysus's band, Heavens Above, couldn't

play because most of the members were groomsmen today. But Medusa recognized one of their songs called "I Promise."

She couldn't help feeling a sense of awe as each groomsman and bridesmaid came down the aisle together, walking slowly and ceremoniously. She felt wistful too. After all, she had hoped to be in this ceremony herself! Aphrodite and Ares were first, then Persephone and Hades, followed by Athena and Heracles. All three goddessgirls looked beautiful in their long white chitons, with orange roses in their hair and golden sandals on their dainty feet.

She glanced at Artemis sitting one row over with her crush, Actaeon. Although she was the only one of the four friends who'd been left out of the wedding, she didn't look at all bothered about it. In fact, if Medusa wasn't mistaken, while everyone's eyes were glued to the ceremony, she was secretly sharpening one of her arrows in her lap with a table knife!

Dionysus and little Andromeda were the sixth of the seven couples. When they passed Medusa's chair, Andromeda waved at her, bouncing with excitement. She looked adorable in her lacy white chiton with flowers twined in her hair. Seeing Medusa, Dionysus sent her a smile, and her heart lifted.

"Ooh, that Dionysus is so cute," she overheard a girl behind her whisper to a friend. She turned and gave the girl the stink eye. "Shhh," she and her snakes hissed. Immediately zipping her lip, the girl nodded, glancing worriedly at Medusa's wiggly hair.

Medusa just sniffed in a superior way and turned back around. The girl was right, though. Dionysus did look cute in his white tunic and new sandals. So cute that

she hardly even noticed when Poseidon and his partner came down the aisle afterward.

It was funny how things worked out sometimes. She was glad Andromeda's dream of being in the wedding had come true, yet a little sad that her own dream had not. She would probably never become immortal. On the bright side, she *had* become a bit more popular, she no longer pined for Poseidon, and she was even beginning to make a few friends. So on balance maybe that wasn't so bad!

Now the music changed slightly, becoming more dramatic. All eyes were on Hera as she glided down the aisle alone, wearing a golden floor-length chiton with a shimmering train that stretched ten feet behind her. Her long gloves had been dyed to match, and she wore a simple gold tiara in her blond hair, which was elaborately styled. The delicate fragrance of her bouquet of lilies, orange blossoms, and pale pink roses lingered as she moved down the aisle and then up the steps to stand beside a beaming Zeus.

Facing her, Zeus took Hera's hand and began to say his vows in a booming voice that had some guests discreetly covering their ears. "I, Zeus, promise to love and adore you forever and ever and always—even if you insist on keeping your job! But everyone here today should know that you're only keeping your job because you like it, and not because I'm poor or a wimp or anything. And after all, look at this amazing wedding you organized here today. You're obviously great at it!"

Hera smiled at him, then parted her lips to speak her vows more softly. "And I, Hera, promise to love and adore you forever and ever and always, and to never complain about scorch marks in the chair cushions or thunderbolt holes in the walls."

Zeus's smile got even wider.

Then the herald came forward to stand behind them, facing the audience. "If anyone here objects to this marriage, speak now or forever be silent." Zeus turned to glare at the audience, his flashing eyes daring anyone to make a peep. The room went completely quiet.

Bzzzz-bzzzz.

At the sudden buzzing sound, everyone looked upward to see a fly zip into the gym through the open ceiling. They all held their breath. Medusa glanced at Athena up on the stage, wondering if this was her mom, Metis, coming to ruin Zeus's wedding. But then the fly just buzzed merrily off, and everyone heaved a sigh of relief.

Zeus's voice boomed out again, "Okay! By the powers vested in me, by me—I now pronounce myself still King of the Gods and Ruler of the Heavens." Then he gazed at Hera, and his voice softened, "And I pronounce Hera to be Queen of the Gods and Co-Ruler of the Heavens. And stepmom to my favorite daughter of all time too!"

He glanced around. Finding Athena, he swept her up in a huge hug and brought her to join him and her new stepmom under the arch. Then he leaned forward and gave Hera a big smooch.

"Awesome wedding!" Zeus roared, smiling over the crowd.

A hearty cheer sounded as hundreds of lovebirds flew upward to form the words "Zeus & Hera" inside a heart shape in midair. (Aphrodite's magical wedding gift.) Then the birds scattered, showering everyone with glittery confetti. Medusa's snakes snapped at it and seemed disappointed when they figured out the confetti wasn't actually snacks.

When Zeus and Hera descended from the stage, it

immediately retracted to reveal the flower-filled heart-shaped pool in the grotto below. From a fountain in its center, water began to spurt high, forming intricate patterns in the air. Poseidon's design, of course. He might be *personally* shallow, but Medusa couldn't deny that his talent with water had depth!

Soon the newly married couple began slicing the wedding cake, which was almost as tall as Zeus himself. The brilliantly colored lovebirds carried numerous small plates of delicious ambrosia-flavored cake to each table. However, the guests barely had time to taste it before Zeus declared, "Let the gift opening begin!"

He and Hera took their seats on two thrones, which had magically floated down from above to settle in front of the fountain. Zeus was as excited as a little kid at a birthday party, beaming from ear to ear as he opened each new gift, then quickly shoved it aside to get to the next. But when he unwrapped a magic thunderbolt from Athena, Medusa could tell it was his favorite present so far, because he immediately decided to try it out.

"How does this thing work?" He shook it, then examined it closely from one end to the other. As he stood and drew back to hurl it, everyone ducked. Fortunately, he aimed it toward the opening in the roof.

Unfortunately, instead of zooming out of the gym, the bolt did a loop-de-loop and sailed toward Perseus's table near the pool instead. With a valiant effort the little boy held out his shield, trying to stop it. But the bolt sliced right through it, stabbing the image of Medusa in the neck and splitting the shield in two.

Ye gods! Medusa's hand automatically flew to her own throat, and she gulped.

Surprised, Perseus dropped the broken shield, and

its two halves tumbled into the pool. Almost immediately the water began to gurgle and bubble.

Whoosh! With an upward splash a small blaze of white and gold zoomed up from the pool. Everyone gasped as it soared toward the ceiling, growing larger and larger, until it finally became a full-grown white horse with mighty golden wings. It caught the wayward thunderbolt in its teeth and winged it back to a delighted Zeus.

"Pegasus?" Medusa heard the murmurs around her, and her brows rose. She'd always thought this magical horse was a myth! Judging by the excited whispers circulating in the room, most of the wedding guests had thought so too. She wasn't sure what strange combination of magic had freed him from her charm—for she was certain that's where he'd come from. But however it had happened, she was just as happy as Zeus to see the beautiful winged horse come to life.

The guy from the *Greekly Weekly News* ran to the stage, sketching away. No doubt the story of this amazing wedding would fill an entire special edition of the *GW* news-scroll tomorrow. And the unexpected arrival of the mythical Pegasus was the icing on the wedding cake!

"Wowza! A living, breathing thunderbolt holder. One that even fetches. What an awesome gift!" Zeus boomed as he stroked the horse's glossy mane. "Who's it from?" His gaze roved over the crowd.

Medusa said nothing. It would be lying to claim that she'd bought the horse for Zeus and Hera. She'd only bought a necklace. For *herself*. Of course, she'd hoped and had sort of believed in its magical powers, but they hadn't turned out as she'd originally planned.

When no one spoke up, the horse's wings began flapping again. It flew once around the domed ceiling and then came straight to Medusa. Gently coming to land before her, Pegasus nuzzled her cheek with his nose. He truly was a magical gift fit for a king, just as she'd wished for yesterday. Noticing something shiny on his wing, she looked closer. It was the golden chain from her necklace, caught on one of his feathers! Carefully she tugged it loose.

"You! Come forth!" Zeus called to her. "You shall be rewarded for this fabulous gift."

"But I didn't—," Medusa started to say. Before she could continue, Pegasus nudged her arm, and then tossed his head toward Zeus. It was like he was telling her to go ahead and claim the reward! Tucking the chain into her pocket, she left her seat and walked over to the thrones. Behind her the kindergarten buddies began swarming around the horse, standing on chairs to pet its muzzle and mane.

When Medusa stood before Zeus, he asked, "Well, mortal, what reward do you choose?"

She didn't have to think about it for even half a second.

233

"I choose immortality!" she replied in a clear voice.

"Done!" Zeus declared just as fast. "I hereby proclaim that tomorrow, for one entire day, you shall be immortal."

Medusa blinked. "I only get one measly day?"

"Is there a problem?" Zeus asked, lifting a bushy red eyebrow.

From beside her she heard Athena murmur, "Don't look a gift horse in the mouth."

Ha! she thought. The real gift horse was Pegasus. But remembering that Athena was the goddessgirl of wisdom, Medusa wisely decided to take her advice. "All right. I accept," she told Principal Zeus. One day was better than nothing!

The band struck up a song then, and Hera and Zeus headed for the dance floor. Hera must've gotten Zeus to take some lessons before the wedding, because he actually didn't look half bad. The other times Medusa had seen him dance, he'd jerked around like a puppet on a string doing something that could only be generously described as a cross between the hula, the tango, and the bunny hop. Soon the wedding guests, young and old, joined in the dancing too. And Pegasus began giving rides to the kids, swooping overhead.

Aphrodite bumped Medusa's arm. "C'mon. Some of us girls are going to dance." Medusa followed her onto the dance floor and wound up next to Dionysus, who was with little Andromeda.

"Did you see me in the wedding?" Andromeda asked, sounding excited.

Medusa nodded. "Mm-hmm. Good job!"

Dionysus grinned at her, dimpling. "Want to join us?"

"Sure." Medusa offered her hand, and he took it in his free one. Holding on to both girls, he twirled them around expertly. A minute later Andromeda ran off for a ride on Pegasus. Artemis and Actaeon seemed to be having a great time organizing the rides and helping kids mount and dismount the magical horse.

Some of the other godboys were dancing now too—Ares with Aphrodite, Heracles with Athena, and Hades with Persephone. Suddenly the music changed and a slow dance began.

Without missing a beat Dionysus pulled Medusa closer. When he put one hand on her waist and took her other hand in his, she didn't object. This was turning out to be the best day of her life! As he whirled her around the floor, someone shouted, "Hey! Hera's going to throw her bouquet."

Pulling away from Dionysus, Medusa watched as Hera tossed her bouquet in a high arc toward a bunch of girls. Keeping her eyes pinned on it, Medusa leaped over chairs, knocking them down, and pushed her way

236

through the crowd. She made a dramatic dive for the bouquet. Catching it midair, she crashed to the ground, hugging it to her chest. *Yes! Victory!*

There was a moment of astonished silence. Sitting up, Medusa realized she had probably just embarrassed herself. But she'd so wanted a bouquet of her very own to remember this magical day. This one would go on her bulletin board for sure.

The silence was broken when Aphrodite and Athena punched their fists in the air and yelled, "Woo-hoo! You go, girl!" From their spots nearby, Artemis and Persephone joined in the cheering. And suddenly other wedding guests were cheering her too.

"Good catch, greenie girl," Dionysus said, appearing at her side to help her up. Another slow song started, and they began to dance again. Medusa held the bouquet in her hand at his shoulder. And when her snakes began to munch on the flowers, she was pleased to note that he didn't seem the least bit weirded out. It made her like him even more.

A week ago she couldn't have dreamed she'd be having so much fun tonight. But now she knew that unrealistic or even impossible dreams *could* come true, just maybe not in the way you expected. That was okay, though, because sometimes you wound up with something even better. Like a crush named Dionysus instead of one named Poseidon. Or an unimaginably great gift for the King of the Gods. Or the chance to be immortal, if only for a day.

Sighing happily, she began to imagine what tomorrow would be like. And slowly, a new episode of the Queen of Mean began to spin itself in her head . . .

The Queen of Mean (episode # 25)

Immortal for a Day!

In this episode the Queen of Mean gets to be a goddess-girl for a whole day. Suddenly she can make the winged sandals fly without any help. So she laces them on and buzzes around the courtyard, doing awesome flips and tricks in midair that no one at MOA has ever seen before!

Then the Queen zooms home to Greece to use her amazing powers to fight evil. (And also to show them off of course!) When she gets there, a seal-herder named Proteus is terrorizing her poor parents. No problem! She whips out her magic cheese and shouts, "Gorgonzola!"

And *poof!*, Proteus is vaporized. Afterward her mom says, "Thank you for saving us, Queen of Mean. You rock!" Her dad grunts in a happy way for once too. And guess what? Turns out that they even hang a picture of the Queen on their wall, bigger than all the others of her sisters.

When the Queen returns to Mount Olympus Academy that night, she is exhausted from her crime fighting. But the four most popular goddessgirls at MOA—Athena, Persephone, Aphrodite, and Artemis—beg her to hang out at the Supernatural Market. Of course she goes! And that cute godboy Dionysus just happens to be there. *And* he just happens to save her a seat by him.

Later the Queen does one last thing before her epic day of being immortal is over. She asks the godboy of blacksmithing, Hephaestus, to forge a sparkly new charm for her Immortalizer necklace chain. Not a GG charm as she has so often longed for. No—this is a very special one-of-a-kind charm. One with the letters: *QoM*.

And only she will ever know what *that* stands for! Ha-ha-ha!

HERE'S A SNEAK PEEK AT . . .

Goddess Girls

SUPER
SPECIAL

THE GIRL GAMES

WE ARE STANDING IN THE COURTYARD OF Mount Olympus Academy," a goddessgirl named Artemis announced to the tour group gathered around her. The seven girls in her group, who were visiting MOΛ for the next few days, followed her gaze. The majestic academy—built of gleaming white stone and surrounded on all sides by dozens of Ionic columns—

stood right behind her at the top of the granite staircase.

Pointing down, Artemis continued. "The white marble tiles beneath your feet were brought here from a quarry in—" Hesitating, she brushed back the dark curls that had fallen across her forehead, and glanced at the official MOA Tour Guide scroll she held in her hands. "Thassos."

"Wherever *that* is," she heard one of the Amazon girls in her group whisper. Her name was Penthesilea and she wore dozens of silver bracelets on both arms. Hippolyta, another Amazon girl, smacked the pine gum she was chewing and gave a big yawn.

All around the courtyard other MOA students were leading other groups of girls on tours too.

It's just my luck to get these two mean Amazon girls in my group, thought Artemis. They wore platform sandals, stood ten inches taller than any of the other girls here, and were known for being bold and brash. Still, they didn't have to be rude!

Artemis's goddessgirl friend Persephone sent her an encouraging smile. She was helping Artemis lead the group, and was always trying to make sure everyone got along.

In truth, Artemis couldn't really blame the Amazons for being bored. These girls had come a long way from schools down on Earth and other realms. And they certainly hadn't traveled here for this lame tour of the academy. They'd come to take part in this weekend's Olympic Games. The very first girls-only games to be exact! A thrill of excitement shot up her spine at the thought of the upcoming competitions.

Although everybody was calling them the Girl Games, their official name was the *Heraean* Games.

Zeus, the principal of MOA, had named them after his new wife, Hera. And it was Hera's bright idea to have MOA students give these tours to visiting girl athletes.

It was a good idea, Artemis supposed, but she didn't have *time* to play tour guide. She had too much other stuff to do to get ready for the games. Like her, these girls would probably rather be off practicing for their own athletic events right now. After all, the games would take place this Saturday—only two days away!

Noticing how stressed Artemis was, Persephone took over as tour guide. "Note the friezes sculpted below the Academy's peaked roof," she said, reading from her scroll. Her slim, pale arm brushed past her long, curly red hair as she lifted her hand overhead, drawing their group's attention to the friezes. Then she led them up the granite staircase and through the academy's enormous bronze front doors.

Artemis followed, thinking of the mega-zillion tasks she still needed to do to make sure that every event would go off without a hitch. These girls-only Olympics had been her idea, and she didn't want them to bomb. How awful would that be? Her stomach tightened just thinking about the possibility.